To Cathy

Lunar

Best wishes

MARTIN TRACEY

Martin

X

Cover artwork by Chris from KUDI-Design
www.kudi-design.com

ISBN: 9798697857175

DEDICATION

For the Lunar Society, who gave even more than they ever knew.

ACKNOWLEDGEMENTS

Thanks as ever to my family.
Special thanks to Simon Blanchett-Parker, Helen Line and
Anita Quick for providing me with a valuable insight into
past life regressions.
Thanks to Louise Dixon, Jax and Bex for ensuring my
words made sense.
Thanks to Peter Iain Roberts for helping to find a cool
name for a gunslinger.
And last but by no means least…
Dear reader, thanks as ever for reading my words. Without
a reader, there is no story to tell.

CHAPTER 1
FIXING A HOLE

The construction worker fell backwards in shock and scurried across the dusty floor like a frightened squirrel might when an unfamiliar presence is upon them.

He swiftly removed his hard hat and protective goggles illustrating the magnitude of what his eyes had seemingly just witnessed. However, the protective part of his brain had been destined to kick in at this point, wired to question anything that defied normality. Even so, he quickly came to realise that his eyes had not deceived him.

Cain had worked on many building developments over the years and it was common place in his profession to joke with his colleagues about discovering such things, never really expecting the scenario to come true.

Yet now it had happened.

During the renovation of Great Barr Hall, Cain had discovered the remains of a human skeleton.

CHAPTER 2
I DON'T WANT TO SPOIL THE PARTY

"Happy birthday once again double-C."

Crystal playfully slapped at Judd's arm. "I told you never to call me that."

"I'm just trying to make you sound cool, Crystal. You know, give you a bit more street-cred. After all, that's yet another year you've gone and notched up since you were born isn't it?"

"Are you looking for another slap, Judd Stone? Only this time it'll come twice as hard."

"Ok, ok. Mrs. Chamberlain it is."

"Now you're making me sound like a school headmistress. Crystal will be just fine, thank you very much."

Judd had taken to calling Crystal Chamberlain, the wife of his best-friend William, by the nickname of double-C in a playful reflection of her initials since their marriage in Las Vegas. In actual fact, it had been a double-wedding with Judd committing himself to Brooke at the exact same Elvis themed ceremony. This act of double commitment highlighted the deep friendship that each couple held for one another.

The crazy weddings had taken place during a tour of pop-star sensation Phoenix. Judd had been employed as her bodyguard at the time. Sharing the life of a bonafide pop star, who liked to party harder than hard, made it easy for the four friends to get caught up in the razzmatazz of it all. Especially in Vegas. Not that either couple had any regrets at getting hitched since returning to a more, shall we say, regular lifestyle. These days Judd was strictly a Private Investigator once again, as sadly his days of being a bodyguard to Phoenix had come to an end.

Phoenix had been certified dead at the age of just twenty-seven, albeit amongst the usual conspiracy fuelled circumstances of an artist passing so young. Nevertheless, and regardless of what had really happened to the talented songstress, Judd found himself surplus to requirements for protecting a pop star who was either dead or who wanted the world to believe she was dead.

In actual fact, as wonderful an experience as it had undoubtedly been, Judd didn't like to talk about his time rubbing shoulders with one of the biggest ever stars on the planet. The media sensed he had answers but whether he did or he didn't, he at least could always protect the Phoenix that he knew and her reputation, even if he could no longer physically protect her.

In truth, the offers of book deals, tabloid serials and taking part in documentaries were at last beginning to dry up. The industry must have finally started to get the message. Judd Stone's stubbornness may have prevented his bank account from growing but at least his integrity and loyalty to Phoenix remained intact. He would always view the time he had spent protecting her as a privilege.

And there were still times when he sorely missed her.

Today, the four friends who had shared that special wedding ceremony in sunny Las Vegas were now stepping out in over-cast Birmingham, England, not long after eating a delicious meal at one of Crystal's favourite canal side restaurants situated between The Mailbox and Gas Street Basin. After all, it had been her birthday so it was only right that she should have chosen the venue.

In spite of his Multiple Sclerosis, William had been determined to walk along Birmingham's canals beside the woman he loved on her birthday, supported by walking sticks as opposed to relying on his wheelchair.

Unfortunately, his noble act of independence had contributed significantly as to why he had fallen into the water of the canal once the shots had been fired. But not before he had handed Brooke a small jiffy bag whilst Crystal and Judd had been engaged in their banter nearby.

"What's this?" She had enquired.

"Just something you may need to give to your husband someday, when I'm no longer around."

"Don't talk like that, William. You'll be around for years to come yet." During that conversation, Brooke could never have guessed how poignant her words would become.

William smiled. "Maybe, but let's just call it a bit of insurance just in case, aye Brooke."

"B... but, I don't understand."

"Shhh. I don't have the time or inclination to discuss it right now. Today is a day for celebration. Just trust me. It makes sense if you have it for safekeeping. I can't give it to lover boy, Judd would lose his head if it wasn't screwed on."

"Ok. Thanks. I think." Brooke could see that William seemed worried about something but the wink of his eye and forced smile of reassurance had underlined that it was not the time to pry. Still curious, Brooke placed the small package into her handbag.

Amidst the panicked screams of visitors to the canals, Judd immediately scanned the area in a desperate attempt to locate the source of the gun shots. His eyes fell onto a figure sitting astride a motorcycle. The helmet was unusual with a flame emblazoned down either side of its shell and frustratingly it covered the facial features of the shooter. Nevertheless, Judd somehow connected with the hidden, cold stare that lay behind the visor, before another round of shots were fired which connected first with Crystal and then Brooke.

In that split second, Judd couldn't decide whether to run to the aid of his wife or to charge head-first at the gunman. The decision was taken from him as he felt a sharp pain enter his stomach. Judd knew it was serious as he found himself hopelessly rooted to the spot and watched the blood spread across the lower area of his shirt. Not long after he passed out, the motorcyclist spun around in the blink of an eye and raced up the ramp out of Gas Street Basin towards his escape into Broad Street.

CHAPTER 3
I'M ONLY SLEEPING

"Mr. Stone, you really should be resting in bed," said the concerned nurse.

"I'm fine," he replied solemnly, holding his wife's hand.

The nurse raised a smile. "I understand. You want to be with your wife, Mr. Stone. Look, I tell you what. I'll draw the curtains so you can have some privacy for five minutes but I will have to be back then to help you return to your bed. Just don't let on to the ward sister or consultant that I've allowed this to happen. We need to get you well too, you know."

"She will she be okay won't she, nurse? I mean, all these wires and stuff, it's a little scary."

The nurse smiled again. "She's strong, Mr. Stone. We are doing all we can but only the consultant can provide you with the answers you seek I'm afraid."

"Look at her innocent face."

"She's beautiful."

"Why did this have to happen to her? It should be me on the life support system, not her."

"I'm sure neither of you deserved any of this... You

should know that the police will want to speak with you soon, Mr. Stone, but we can try and delay them if you're not ready."

"Thanks. It's ok, I know how it works. I'm an ex-copper myself. The thing is I really don't know what I can tell them. I have no idea whatsoever why this happened. I still have friends in the police and I'm sure they're already out there looking for whoever did this. Anyway, when I get out of here, I'll personally make sure I get even with whoever is responsible for putting my wife in this state. In fact, I really feel like I need to do something now." Judd was becoming a little animated.

"I understand how you must be feeling, Mr Stone, but please, you must keep calm. You still have a gunshot wound yourself."

"I'm fine. I want to discharge myself, right now please nurse."

"Perhaps in a few days Mr. Stone. You really are not well enough at the moment. Just be there for your wife right now. She's the one who needs you."

"I've got to do something. Anything. I feel so useless."

"I do understand, Mr. Stone."

Judd composed himself. He knew that the nurse was talking sense and meant well. "Please, call me Judd. Sorry, I should have told you that earlier."

"Ok, Judd. Nice name by the way."

"Thanks. Can she hear me?"

"Every word."

"Then she knows I can at least deliver on my promise to her." Judd kissed his wife's hand.

The nurse gave a frown, intrigued as to the promise that Judd wished to fulfil.

Judd grimaced as he stood up, the wound which once held a bullet remained stubborn to the strongest of painkillers. He stroked Brooke's hair and tucked a strand gently behind her ear as the machine beeped and her closed eyelids fluttered. "Even once I'm allowed out of here, I'll come and see you every single day until you wake up my darling. Now, we both know there's something you want me to do and despite what I may have said before, I've decided I'm gonna do it. For you. When you wake up, I'll be a changed man." Then, Judd softly kissed his wife on the forehead as she slept.

CHAPTER 4
YOU HAVE BEEN LOVED

Fortunately, the medics decided that Judd had made enough of a recovery to be discharged from hospital in time to attend the funerals of his two dearest friends. Not that anything could have kept him away from paying his respects.

It seemed that he had been the lucky one, which nagged away at his residual guilt complex. Brooke remained on a life support machine but at least he had hope where she was concerned. It was hard to fully comprehend that he would never see the faces of William and Crystal again.

Judd had already decided that the very next day after the funeral he was going to deliver on his promise to Brooke. He was determined that something positive had to come out of his wife's desperate state of illness.

He considered if he had ever told her how much of an inspiration she had been to him?

Had he told her often enough how much he loved her? And had he told his friends the same thing often enough too?

Now, Judd could only hope that he had.

The realisation had hit him like a juggernaut, life really was too short. Judd had come to realise that no one could foresee what was waiting around the corner for them, including himself.

The turnout for the funeral had been exceptional. William and Crystal had clearly been a very much loved and respected couple. The fact that they had been taken in such tragic and needless circumstances only served to fuel the heartache.

Even though William had no longer been a serving police officer, police vehicles formed part of the cortege and Judd had reunited with members of the force one more time to be one of the pallbearers. Any pain still remaining from his injury wasn't going to stop him lifting the coffin of his dear friend. Another pallbearer had been his and William's close friend DSI Ben Francis.

Sab Mistry, Judd and William's former colleague in CID, had flown over from the States to pay her respects. For the most part, Judd had shared a table at the wake with his friend Sab and William's sister Tilda. Tilda was a huge George Michael fan and she had arranged for the song "You Have Been Loved" to be played at the service. The lyrics of the song had been fitting for both William and Crystal.

"Why did this have to happen Judd?" said Tilda as she hugged her coffee cup.

"I'll find out, Tilda. I promise you." Judd looked at the sister of his best friend and felt an overwhelming sense of sorrow for her. Tilda's husband had been brutally murdered by the crazed offspring of Charles Manson no less and now here she was having to relive the raw emotions of such a hideous crime all over again with the slayings of her brother and his wife.

"God knows we made enemies over the years," said Sab. "It's impossible not to in our line of work, but William had been out of the game for a few years, so why now?"

"Perhaps they were after me and William," said Judd. "Crystal and Brooke had just been collateral damage. Out of all of us I'd say that I'd be the most likely target considering what I've been embroiled in in the past."

"Don't you dare start one of your guilt trips on us, Judd," said Sab with good intent. "You can't blame yourself for this one."

"Sab is right, Judd," said Tilda. "If this was a professional hit it was clearly meant for my brother and his wife. I think it is you and Brooke that were the collateral damage."

"Well at least William was right about one thing," said Judd. "He always sworn that he wouldn't let MS kill him."

"He did, didn't he?" said Tilda, forcing a smile. "Well that's something, I suppose."

"Do you think that someone could have been upset by William's and Crystal's research?" offered Sab.

"I can't see why," said Judd. "As far as I know their primary aim was to try and find a way to cure MS. Who would be pissed off by that?"

"Those who don't want a cure," said Tilda, taking Judd a little by surprise. "Ruthless and capitalist drug companies for instance. And who knows what other secrets William and Crystal may have unlocked during their research. My brother seemed very anxious on the telephone of late, but every time I asked him if anything was wrong, he would quickly shut me down. It felt like he was definitely hiding something."

"Did he ever appear cagey to you, Judd?" asked Sab.

Judd thought for a moment as he finished the last gulps of his pint of bitter. Wiping his mouth with the back of his hand he answered Sab's question. "Come to think of it he did a bit. Both William and Crystal actually. They certainly hadn't wanted to talk shop at Crystal's birthday meal, but I had assumed that had just been because it wasn't the time and place."

"Maybe, but think about it, Judd," said Tilda. "Think how passionate they both usually were to speak of their breakthroughs. Think how animated they would become when they spoke of their progress on understanding the power of the human brain. They were increasingly making science fiction into science fact and that can actually upset a lot of people. People who benefit from the status quo and all that is accepted around us."

"Then like I said earlier, Tilda. I'll find out."

CHAPTER 5
REHAB

While Brooke Stone lay on a life support machine, her husband was about to deliver on his promise to his wife.

However, he very nearly didn't.

Judd had opened and closed the entrance door of the 1970's-built community centre a total of five times before he finally, and gingerly, entered the foyer and then walked through the internal double-doors into the room.

The wooden floor hosted a herringbone pattern and was typical of the construction style of the times. The space was vast, yet the collection of orange coloured plastic chairs had been placed centrally and in a circle like some modern-day scaled down Stonehenge. To Judd, the chairs seemed at least a mile away from where he had entered and now stood rooted to the spot.

Judd Stone had traded punches with the hardest of men. He had even killed people without batting an eyelid. Yet here he was, terrified more than ever, to simply take the short walk across the floor and join the circle.

His nervousness eased slightly when a friendly voice called out from a rotund lady sitting on one of the chairs.

She was obviously well-rehearsed in trying to make new members to the group feel welcome., but when Judd accepted her invitation to join proceedings, the distance didn't just look like it had been a mile to walk, it also felt like it too.

Judd trod slowly and wearily.

In spite of the rotund lady's warm smile, the other members of the group stared at Judd as if he had two heads. Or at least it felt that way to him.

"Please, take a seat," offered the kind lady, her smile never faltering. "My name's Sandra but all my friends call me Sandy, so you can call me Sandy."

Judd couldn't help but return a smile. This woman's warm personality was infectious.

Without removing his hands from his coat pockets, Judd flopped down on one of the orange chairs between a middle-aged woman with wonky spectacles and a quiff-crested youngster who Judd thought could benefit from eating a decent meal.

"Ok I think we are ready to start," said Sandy addressing the group. "I'll begin by just reminding everyone, and for the sake of our new members, what it is we try and achieve here at 'Fighting Gambling Together'. This is a non-judgmental forum where we each discuss our experiences, challenges and hopes as we build the blocks together to step away from our addictions of compulsive gambling. Are we all comfortable with that, everybody?"

A few amenable grunts echoed through the large space of the hall as well as some more audible affirmations. There were lots of heads nodding too.

Sandy's eyes fell squarely on Judd, which made him shuffle a little in his chair with awkwardness.

"So, what is your name, friend?"

"I thought this was meant to be anonymous?" replied Judd, not feeling too thrilled at being the centre of attention.

Sandy smiled. "It's a fair point to make, but what we

mean by anonymous is that what is discussed here, amongst the group, is treated as strictly confidential by us all. However, with an individual's blessing it can at times seem a little silly not to share the success stories of what we achieve. But please be assured that no information attributed to you can ever be shared without your approval. Sharing our names amongst the group helps us to create that all important supportive bond, but it's fine if you want to use a pseudonym if that makes you feel more comfortable."

"No, it's fine. Hi everyone, my name's Judd."

Sounds of "Hey Judd…. hello Judd…welcome Judd," filled the room.

Sandy spoke again through her smile. "Yes indeed, welcome Judd. Perhaps you could let the group know what brought you to FIGHT this evening?"

"My wife wanted me to come."

"Ok. Well that's great that she seems so supportive, Judd, but what about how you're feeling? Did you want to come, yourself? Nothing can be achieved until you and your innermost self recognises that you have a gambling addiction. Along with self-recognition there also has to be a willful desire to recover."

Judd thought for a second. "I get it. I'm happy to admit that I have a problem. My wife's, err, current situation has just made me see things a little clearer that's all. I want to get well for her. She's my inspiration."

"Then once again, Judd. Welcome."

CHAPTER 6
HELP!

She walked into Judd's Rotunda building office carrying a musical instrument case that was almost as big as her.

"Hello, are you in a band?" enquired Judd.

"Oh, the case? It's a bit of a giveaway isn't it? I'm on my way to rehearsal. I'm a cellist in the CBSO."

Nice accent, thought Judd. He placed it as being perhaps Italian or Spanish. "CBSO?"

"Sorry, City of Birmingham Symphony Orchestra."

"Ahh, so you're a posh musician?"

The joke was lost on the cellist as she frowned.

"Never mind," smiled Judd. "Please take a seat, how can I help you? I assume you require my help?"

"Si, Senor."

Spanish. "Do you have time for a tea or coffee perhaps?"

"I have time for an espresso, thank you."

Judd called for Yasmin, his assistant and Sab's younger sister, who appeared swiftly at the doorway to Judd's office. Yasmin please could you rustle up a small coffee. No milk."

"You mean an espresso?" Said Yasmin rolling her eyes. She was a first-class PA but her interpersonal skills would forever be found wanting. To be fair to Judd, he hadn't been fully aware of what their coffee machine could produce.

"Yes, an espresso and just the usual for me."

Judd offered the cellist a seat. She accepted and sat down opposite Judd after placing the cello case against one of Judd's bookcases. Briefly scanning the titles of some of the books helped to relax her.

"Fortunately, I see from your books that you have an open mind, Mr. Stone."

"Please call me Judd. Miss err?"

"Moreno. Vina Moreno."

"Pleased to meet you Vina Moreno, cellist of CBSO."

Vina smiled for the first time during the encounter. "Gracias."

Judd was puzzled at her nervousness. "Tell me how I can I help you Miss Moreno?"

"Please, call me Vina," she said bringing a strand of dark hair behind her ear.

"How can I help you, Vina?"

"I need the services of a private detective."

"Well you've certainly come to the right place."

Just then Yasmin entered the room with the drinks, placed them on the desk rather heavily and left again without speaking a word.

"You were saying, Vina?"

"In all honesty, it's not that easy for me to say. However, I must for the sake of my own sanity."

Judd was becoming increasingly intrigued. "Please do go on. Believe me, I have experienced some very incredible things in recent years that would make your toes curl, so I'm not easily shocked."

"Toes curl?"

"Never mind. It's just an English expression."

"Oh, ok."

"Please, Vina. Continue, and remember what I said. I'm not easily shocked."

"I see things… what I mean is… how do you say? I have visions, Mr Stone. Judd."

"What type of visions?"

"They are not always clear but they mainly come in my dreams, when I'm asleep. They have always unnerved me but I've got used to living with them. They have never made a lot of sense, until now that is."

"Why now?"

Vina took a sip of her espresso before answering. "Are you aware of the skeleton that was recently found in Great Barr Hall?"

"I am, yes. Some of my former colleagues from the Police Force became involved for a short time but as soon as the body was discovered to be from the eighteenth century, they soon lost interest. I mean, even the famous Jack the Ripper murders remain unsolved and they came much later."

"Well, I need you to be interested Judd."

Judd sat forward to accentuate his attention. "I'm all ears, Vina. But the discovery of this body isn't exactly a King in a car park phenomenon as far as I can tell. Why does this particular find interest a cellist from Spain?"

"Because I think the body could be me?"

Judd looked a little stunned. What on earth was the woman saying? How could the skeletal discovery have been Vina Moreno when she was sitting right in front of him?

"Please don't think I'm crazy," said Vina.

"No, no of course I don't. Perhaps a little confused. Please elaborate, you have my full attention."

"These dreams I speak of, I've had all of my life. As I said, they never used to make much sense. But now I know that my music guided me to Birmingham as my destiny, so that I can begin to understand. With the discovery of the skeleton, it's starting to make some sense to me. But I need more and the police, as you say, are not interested in understanding who the victim is."

"I did read somewhere that the discovery is thought to have been a murder, obviously from a number of centuries ago."

"I would like you to find out who the victim of this murder is Judd, because I'm convinced it is me in a former life."

"Oh, I see." At least Judd thought he did.

"Have you heard of past life regression, Judd?"

"Yes, though I'm hardly an expert."

"Well I've tried many things over the years to try and understand what it is that I see. For example, I've tried dream analysis and meditation but they never really revealed a lot. But recently I began to undergo past life regressions and they have really helped to bring some clarity to my dreams."

"This sounds really interesting," encouraged Judd genuinely.

"Past-life regression hasn't told me specifically who I was back then, but when I have regressed, I have been able to see a very rural landscape with a church in the distance. However, right next to me there is also a chapel which hosts a diamond brick design. This chapel is near a very beautiful and grand house.

"The house itself has an arched doorway and this doorway is very gothic in appearance. I know only through my regression that I am familiar with the house's strawberry hill architectural style; this is not something I would ordinarily know.

"Other times I often find myself sitting in a large dining room with the smells of meat and potatoes cooking. I sit at the table with many men, no women, and they dress more smartly than most. Curiously the accents vary and I recognise at least one of them to be Scottish.

"The house has beautiful landscaped gardens and even a lake nearby.

"It is only now, through the discovery of the skeleton and the recent publicity that it has attracted, that I am sure that it is Great Barr Hall where I have been during my regressions."

Judd took a deep breath to help process the information. "Wow, this is truly fascinating, Vina."

"You don't think I'm mad?"

"Not for a second."

Vina looked relieved. "Good, because it's about to get a little crazier."

Judd smiled reassuringly. "I can't wait. Please, do go on."

"Well, there are also a few, how do you say, items that dominate my thoughts and they have always featured in my dreams…" Vina hesitated. "You really don't think I'm crazy?"

"No, please. I'm really intrigued. I'm hanging on your every word, Vina."

"I see a full moon and a vicious dog. Why, I can't explain. I also see a woman, but she is in portraits only. I do not know her personally, but I am aware that she is a female saint. St Margaret of Antioch.

"As well as visions I experience powerful smells, like the smell of musk sometimes. In the dining room I smell cooked food, but I also get a contrasting smell that I can only describe as red-hot metal or something like that.

"All of my senses seem very much alive during my regressions. The scariest part is when I start to feel overwhelming pain in my body coupled with an almighty sense of claustrophobia. I know that I must have come to harm in this past life and this is always at the point that I wake up – whether I'm sleeping naturally or during a regression.

"So, perhaps you can understand how I became very interested when I learned of the discovery of this skeleton that had been found in a confined space in Great Barr Hall?"

"Yes, indeed. Particularly as you have been having this sensation of claustrophobia and the way the body had been stored. Listen Vina, I'd have to research further some of the things that you are describing but I can certainly recognise parallels with Great Barr Hall. You see, I know that the location of the victim's interment has stirred a lot of local curiosity and raised questions about the Lunar Society."

"The Lunar Society?"

"You've not heard of them?"

Vina shook her head.

"Well, I reckon the Lunar Society are the gathering of men that you are describing in the dining room."

"Really?"

"Yes. They were a bunch of chaps that would use the light of the full moon to guide them to the places where they would choose to meet, Great Barr Hall being one of them. Soho House about three miles on from Great Barr in Handsworth is another one.

"The Lunar Society were a collective of brilliant minds made up of scientists, entrepreneurs, philosophers, industrialists and innovators of the time. You may have heard of James Watt for example? Watt was a member of the Lunar Society who revolutionised the wide use of steam engines amongst other things. He was Scottish by the way so maybe he is one of the voices that you heard speak. None of this may sound very exciting and perhaps even a little geeky, Vina, but the Lunar Society were to innovative industrialisation, manufacturing and engineering as to what The Beatles were to music. Or in your case, what Mozart and Beethoven were to music."

"I may be a classical musician but just like any other musician I still dig the Beatles. This Lunar Society sound pretty special too, but for reasons other than music."

"They certainly have a lasting and important legacy, but this discovery of the skeleton has now placed a shadow over their success because people are suggesting they must have known something about the murder."

"Do you know what, Judd? You talking about them now makes things even clearer for me. I knew that you were the right person to help me."

"You've really never heard of The Lunar Society."

"No."

"I guess there's no reason why you should necessarily, I'm not sure if the Industrial Revolution is on the Spanish school curriculum."

"Outside of music I was never really much interested in other subjects."

"Fair enough. PE was the only subject I was ever interested in, but I do remember learning about the Lunar Society in History. I'm certainly no expert on them though.

"PE?"

"Physical Education. Sports."

"Ahh, ok."

"Listen Vina, personally I believe what you have told me about your dreams and this past life regression stuff, but is it possible that you could just be recalling events that you've read or heard about? I could research this murder, but I can't guarantee that I can prove that it was you in a previous life. I don't want to take your money just to put a name to a body that was, let's be frank, killed centuries ago. Who really cares?"

Vina reacted somewhere between desperate and annoyed. "I care. I know it is me from a previous life. No question. You are a private investigator, so I want to hire you to find out what my name was. I have the money to pay you. It'll be worth it to me."

"I really do sympathise, but the thing is Vina, I'm pretty busy already. I have a very personal matter that I need to investigate and that's going to take up a lot of my time. I'd love to help but I'm not sure that I'm prepared to spend a lot of hours on an age-old case."

Vina looked down at the floor.

"I'm sorry, Vina," said Judd. "I really am."

"Well what if I told you that the dreams I have been having have evolved lately? They are pointing at something very scary and very important that is happening today, never mind hundreds of years ago. What if I pay you to solve a very real case that is happening right now? But only if you promise to holistically help me with the murder of Great Barr Hall as well. There may be a connection, somehow."

"*The Murder of Great Barr Hall*. Got a good ring to it that has Vina. Like a book or a film. Or both. But what do you mean something happening now?"

"Like I said. I need you to investigate something that is happening right now."

"Well I guess that depends on how serious it is, like I said I'm very busy investigating something that is very personal to me."

"Well is my 17-year-old cousin being in danger serious enough for you?"

CHAPTER 7
HELLO, GOODBYE

It was all the bait that Judd had needed. Once Vina had explained that her younger female cousin could genuinely be in danger, coupled with Vina's visions of her being killed, he felt duty bound to get involved.

Judd's thought processes could often take a ludicrous journey towards their conclusions. Based on the overwhelming guilt that he still felt for other women that had featured in his life and had come to harm, Judd felt that if he were to walk away now and something were to happen to Vina's cousin, he would always believe it to have been his fault!

However, he wasn't entirely sure where to begin in finding the missing girl. He decided to venture over to Great Barr to see if solving a centuries-old murder on behalf of the same client could somehow help him join the dots.

Judd's hunch had told him that through her past-life regressions, dreams and visions, Vina must have been a catalyst for everything connecting. But just what that connection was he was yet to discover.

Judd steered his car around the huge traffic roundabout, which was known locally as the Queslett island, and resisted the urge to pull over and frequent the betting shop that caught his eye opposite the supermarket.

Not long after he spotted the swinging sign of the Cat and Fiddle pub, not surprisingly depicting a cat playing a fiddle. The pub, which almost resembled a large house with its sloping tiled roof, was nestled at the top of the Park Farm estate, which was also close to the area of Great Barr known as Pheasey. Other signs belonging to the pub advertised its ability to provide televised sports and advertised the value-for-money meal deals that were on offer.

In his experience, Judd realised that a public house was always a good place to start when wanting to take advantage of knowledge that could only be uniquely harboured by the local community.

He had chosen the lounge over the bar and in doing so he had needed to make his way through a group of smokers standing in the outside smoking zone who were blocking that particular entrance. They allowed Judd through without challenge. Once inside he approached the bar and ordered a draft Irish stout.

He scanned the room as the barmaid allowed his three-quartered poured stout to settle before she topped it up to its maximum level. Judd was pleased that she had poured it the way it was meant to be poured. It wasn't a technique that was utilised in every pub sadly – unless you happened to be in Ireland of course.

Judd was searching for potential candidates to speak with and initially spotted a couple of families who were dining. Not wanting to interrupt their eating experience he spotted three ladies sitting by the window, one of the few seating areas positioned away from the TV screens that were currently revealing the latest sports news.

Once his pint of stout had been perfected, he accepted the glass from the barmaid, paid her the cash and swaggered over towards them.

"May I join you?" asked Judd.

"Sure, as long as you keep our drinks flowing," answered the only woman of the three who was sporting a short haircut.

"Fair enough," smiled Judd. "Will another bottle of prosecco do?"

"That'll do nicely," answered another woman with dark hair. "As long as you're not some weirdo."

"Excuse me?" Judd retained his smile.

"Only I can't help noticing that the pub isn't that busy, yet you've made a point of coming all the way over to us. I must say, I am a little curious."

The short-haired woman spoke again. "Come on Lesley, he's only human. He's bound to want to sit with us, isn't he?"

Judd laughed. "Well you ladies certainly know how to speak your mind. Don't worry Lesley, I'm not a weirdo. Believe it or not I'm actually a Private Investigator and I'm hoping that you can help me with something. Here's my business card." Judd handed a card to each of the women and whilst they digested the contents, he signaled to the barmaid to bring over a bottle of prosecco.

"Well hello, Judd Stone P.I. Sounds pretty cool actually. I'm Lois, you've met Lesley and Joanne. How can we help?" Now all three ladies had spoken.

Judd sat down as the barmaid placed a fresh ice bucket and bottle of prosecco on the table.

"How much is that, please?" asked Judd.

"£11.99."

Judd pulled out his wallet, skipped over the fifty-pound note which depicted the portraits of James Watt and Matthew Boulton, and handed the barmaid a five and ten-pound note. "Keep the change."

"Cheers."

"Did we forget to mention the white rum chasers, Judd," smiled Joanne.

"Here's another tenner," said Judd returning to his wallet. "White rums all round, please."

"Sure thing," answered the barmaid.

"Actually, swap mine to a Vodka," said Lesley. The barmaid nodded, hoping that was the end of the evolving order.

Judd returned his attention to the three ladies and placed a photo of a young woman with olive skin and dark hair on the table. "Have you seen this girl?"

"She's pretty," said Lois.

"Yes, she is, and missing sadly."

"That's terrible," said Joanne. "Have you tried reaching out on social media? I can place a picture in a group I manage called 'The Cool Dudes' if you like? Unfortunately, I don't recognise her? Do either of you two?"

"No, sorry," answered Lois and Lesley almost in unison.

Judd sighed. "Never mind, I knew it was a long shot. She only lived in Birmingham for a short time, with her cousin. Her cousin has used social media to try and locate her, or so she tells me, but so far it hasn't helped. As a PI, I have to be a bit more discreet with my enquiries."

"Sounds like you're a cool dude?" said Lesley. "Hey, he could join the group, Joanne."

Judd smiled. "Are you flirting with me, Lesley?"

"I'll have you know that we are all attached women and we are all very happy, Mr. Stone."

Judd smiled once more. "What, attached to each other?"

"You wish," said Lesley. These ladies were good fun and he appreciated the banter.

"I wouldn't want to impose on either your cool dudes' group or of course on you 'spoken for' ladies."

"I wouldn't worry yourself, mate. Lesley was the life and soul of our thirty-year school reunion and she didn't even go to the same school as Joanne and me," said Lois.

Once he'd finished laughing at that latest anecdote,

Judd placed the photograph back into his pocket. "So, what do you think about this body that's been found up at Great Barr Hall?"

"It was a bit of a shock to be honest," offered Lois.

"Oh, I don't know," said Joanne. "I wasn't that surprised when you hear about some of the stories that have happened at Maggie's?"

"Maggie's?" enquired Judd.

"St Margaret's Hospital. Maggie's was built on the grounds in and around Great Barr Hall. It was known back then as a Mental Asylum; I know, not very PC terminology by today's standards but I'm just saying how it was. There's always rumours flying about around here about its history, including many an intriguing tale I've heard in this very pub."

"Really?" said Judd. "Sounds interesting."

"Some of the patients got out into the community you see. They were either allowed out for rehabilitation or the ones who were considered more dangerous sometimes escaped. Either way there are rumours of these patients committing the most appalling local murders. However, the more sinister rumours are those involving the treatment of the patients themselves."

"What do you mean? That they could have been victims too?" asked Judd.

Joanne took a sip from her glass of prosecco before continuing. "Remember Maggie's was erected in 1918 and attitudes and regulations weren't what they are today. Lord only knows what went on behind those closed doors over the decades, but I reckon those acres of woods around the Great Barr Hall estate hold some very dark secrets."

Lesley joined in. "My nana used to tell me some very scary stories about that place. I don't know if it was just a deterrent to keep us away from there, I mean a kid could have easily gotten lost in those grounds and come to harm by a mysterious character lurking about. I tell you what though, she was bloody convincing. No kid in the know would enter that place for all the chocolate in Bournville."

"Do you reckon there's some 'unofficial' graves over there, then?" explored Lois, making inverted commas in the air with her fingers.

"Definitely," answered Joanne. "That place would have been a haven for any of Maggie's staff who got off on abusing the patients, or worse, whilst wanting to remain undetected."

"This all sounds fascinating and pretty chilling I have to say, but is there any proof?" asked Judd.

"Some, but to be honest mainly rumour," answered Joanne. "Just urban legends, perhaps. Who knows? You're the PI, mate perhaps you can find out for certain."

Judd smiled. "Fair enough, I'll bear it in mind. I think I need to start by heading on up to where there has definitely been a murder with a confirmed discovery of a body. Great Barr Hall." Judd finished off the remains of his creamy stout and placed the glass down on the table.

"I'll tell you what, Judd. I'll send you an email to the address on your business card," said Joanne. "You can reply with an attachment of the girl's picture. I'll create a poster and I'll put it up in the Community centre where I run my Autism Supporters Group. There are people going in and out of there all the time."

"Thanks. I really appreciate that. Every little helps but to be honest from what I know so far, she could be absolutely anywhere on the planet. I won't go into detail but she's been rubbing shoulders with the wrong sort of people. Her cousin thinks she has fallen in with a bad crowd. Her name is Rosa Moreno by the way, should you hear anything on the off chance."

"No problem," said Joanne. "If you've driven here, you're much better off leaving your car on the pub car park and walking up to the hall. It's much easier on foot than driving.

"Turn right when you get outside the pub. Head up Waverley Avenue, turn left at the top and then about a hundred yards or so on your right you'll come to a passage between two detached houses on Park Farm Road. They knocked a house down to allow access to the newer estate. I forget what the estate is called now but that's not important. You'll stroll past a black lamppost, the sort that Mr Tumnus would like to meet under, then once you're amongst the new properties keep heading right and you'll see how you can enter the land where Great Barr Hall stands."

"Be careful though," said Lois. "The new estate is called Nether Hall by the way, and you need to cut straight through its recent constructions. If you buy into what Joanne's been telling you you'll be walking on unmarked graves."

"It's very likely," said Joanne.

"I'm sure I'll be fine. Thanks for your help ladies. Enjoy the rest of your drinks, I can see the barmaid is on her way over with them."

CHAPTER 8
THERE'S A PLACE

The walk took a little longer than Judd had anticipated. He found himself walking through the two separate and contrasting housing estates to reach Great Barr Hall. Both estates were very different in design, each one illustrating the respective time period of their creation.

As he strolled through Nether Hall, the more contemporary housing estate of the two, he found himself asking the question – "Don't they build houses with gardens anymore?" Perhaps he was in no position to throw stones in glass houses considering he lived in an apartment, but he would always make sure that his faithful dog Mr Mustard received enough exercise. Most of the time that would be in nearby Cannon Hill Park. He liked to attend the poignant memorial that had been raised for Cassie, Olive and Kez, the three daughters of Birmingham who had been so cruelly taken by macabre serial killer Gareth Banks aka The Crucifier.

It had been Judd who had eventually captured Banks and thus avenged the girls' untimely and needless deaths. Each time he and Muzzy entered the park he would always take the time to stop by the memorial within their Garden of Remembrance and pay his respects to them.

Judd loved living in The Rotunda at the heart of the city of Birmingham, but one day he would perhaps like a house with a garden, especially if he and Brooke were to ever get around to raising a family. He knew that Brooke was keen on the idea, probably keener than he was if he was being honest with himself. He just always seemed too busy to contemplate having a kid or two in tow. But one day, yes, he would like a small family.

Judd understood that Nether Hall had been built on part of the grounds of Great Barr Hall and more recently St Margaret's Hospital. Lois's reference to him walking over unmarked graves crossed his mind more than once as he strolled amongst the houses.

Eventually, Judd reached a metal defence barrier that had clearly been erected to separate the housing estate from the designated path to the Great Barr Hall area. It allowed pedestrians to enter at a particular access point whilst acting as a defence against any motorised vehicles from gaining entrance. Painted black, with the odd bit of etched graffiti from the local youths, the defence barrier wasn't the most pleasant looking contraption to the eye. It's erection on cracked tarmac found Judd hoping that this wasn't going to be a sign of a dreary walk ahead. But he needn't have worried. Judd soon pleasantly discovered that it wasn't a dreary walk at all, and in actual fact the barrier had served its purpose well to assist with an enjoyable environment not plagued by traffic or fumes. Judd did however notice the sound of the nearby M6 motorway, which carried on the breeze and cut through the song of blackbirds. But even this wasn't enough to compromise the surrounding beauty.

In fact, it was almost as if Judd had entered another world altogether. Not quite Narnia status but he could be forgiven for forgetting that beyond the dense woodland and blackberry brambles lay north Birmingham suburbia.

Growing up in Birmingham himself, Judd knew of the Great Barr district, yet in all his years he had never realised that this enchanting place had ever existed. It truly was a hidden gem.

Within a few captivating minutes he had reached Great Barr Hall. Straight away he could recognise some of the features that Vina had described to him, most notably the Gothic arched doorway surrounded by the most impressive sculptured décor and the adjacent chapel with the diamond-bricked pattern. Setting eyes on the building for the first time he hadn't realised that the roof of Great Barr Hall was akin to a castle structure and this certainly added to its charm. However, its charm was currently compromised and Judd had to look beyond the various obstructions of a building site to connect with the hall's potential.

Moments earlier when Judd had turned the corner of the meandering pathway, the hall's magnificence had struck him instantly including the unexpected backdrop of a lush green hill above the castle-like roof. Yet he had been a little taken aback at the acute state of disrepair of the building. Scaffolding and plastic sheeting clung to its walls, hiding its inner beauty, and he could only hope that the building work being undertaken was going to bring the once magnificent building somewhere back to its former glory.

Judd turned to his right momentarily and spotted that once past the hall, the pathway forked in two beneath the shadows of a prominent American redwood tree that stood majestically amongst the equally impressive silver birches. Where either path led to was impossible to tell due to the vast woodland and curvature of the paths, but to Judd, they certainly looked inviting. He surmised that they led to more unexpected beauty but he also wondered what sinister secrets the land beyond could hold considering some of the stories he had now heard about Maggie's? Anyway, that particular walk would have to wait for another day.

The hall had been cordoned off by temporary wire fencing hosting the obligatory display of signs designed to alert people to hazards and warning them to 'keep out'. Yet it was still possible to see what was going on in and around the hall.

Construction workers wearing high visibility vests and hard hats were scattered amongst the scaffolding undertaking various tasks, although to the right of the hall there was a temporary caravan in situ that Judd could see was being utilised as a rest area. Sitting outside the tatty old caravan on deck chairs were a small group of workers each supping on their own mug of legendary 'builders tea'. One of the workers, a large man with a long ginger beard, broke away from the group and headed over towards Judd.

"Can I help you mate?" he said through the fence, followed by a swig from his gigantic mug.

"Hi there, I don't mean to intrude on your break but I'm just interested to learn a bit more about the skeleton that was discovered here not so long ago," replied Judd.

"You're not another fucking journalist, are you?"

"No mate. Not me. My name's Judd Stone, I'm a private investigator. Look, here's my card." Judd passed his business card through the wire fencing and the bearded man took it from him and studied the text for a couple of seconds before replying.

"Why would a PI be interested in such a finding now? Like you said, it was skeleton that was discovered not a fresh body. I doubt that you can catch the killer, he'll be long gone mate. Dead himself in fact."

"True, but my client has very good reasons for me to solve this mystery even though the death occurred so many centuries ago. There's also a possibility that it could lead to the disappearance of a young girl."

"Really? In that case you'd better come in. We'll have to get you kitted up in some protective gear, safety regs I'm afraid."

"Of course, no bother."

"I also need you to stay away from the main site, luckily for you Cain is currently on his tea-break. It was Cain who found the skeleton, you see. Proper shit him up it did too, I can tell you. I'll introduce you to him. You can use the inside of the van if you want a bit of privacy."

"Thanks, I appreciate it."

Judd soon discovered that the inside of the caravan was as unkempt as the outside.

"Fancy a brew?" offered Cain.

Looking at the state of the tea spoons and unwashed mugs piled up in the sink, not to the mention the bottle of milk that probably hadn't seen the inside of a fridge since its purchase, Judd respectably declined.

"No thanks mate, I've not long had a nice stout at the pub down the road."

"Nice that you can drink whilst on duty. I'm clearly in the wrong profession. How can I help ya?"

"I'm investigating the finding of the skeleton here at Great Barr Hall so that I can hopefully discover what happened to the poor sod all those years ago. I understand it was you who came across the remains, Cain."

"Yeah, nearly bloody shit myself. Twenty-five years I've been doing this job and never have I come across anything like that before."

"I can imagine. It must have been a bit of a shock for you."

"It was, mate. To be honest though I don't know how I can help you. It was just a pile of bones really. The face had long gone."

"Was the skeleton in any clothing?"

"Yes, it was actually. The clothes had disintegrated a great deal with time but I could still make out that the poor lass was wearing a dress. A heavily blood-stained dress at that. God knows what she went through."

"Well for a start that's already interesting and helpful.

Thanks, Cain."

"No problem."

"Where about was she buried?"

"I wouldn't call it a burial as such. I found her bricked up in a wall. It looks like she was placed in a small cupboard and then the door way was bricked up."

"Mmmm, that could have either been opportune or a lot more sinister," said Judd.

Cain's hazel-coloured eyes narrowed. "Why's that?"

"I'm wondering was witchcraft at play."

Cain's eyes soon widened again. "Witchcraft? Fuck."

"Superstition was rife in centuries of long ago. Cats for instance were often buried in the walls of cottages and houses. It was believed that cats were a sign of good luck and by killing them and placing them in the walls of the home it meant that they could ward off evil spirits. The cat was offered as a blood sacrifice, you see."

"Blimey, do you think this poor lass could have been a blood sacrifice too then?

"Maybe. It's certainly possible, Cain. To solve a crime like this I have to keep an open mind and explore all possibilities that were akin to the times."

Cain removed his hard hat and ran his fingers through his grey-peppered hair before placing the hat back on his head again. The manoeuvre seemed to allow time for the builder to digest Judd's words and help them to sink in.

Judd continued with his chilling history lesson. "You may have heard of the Pendle Witch trials which happened in Lancashire. In the early seventeenth century a few villagers of Pendle were actually executed because the local folk believed them to be witches."

"Yeah that does ring a bell. I think I have heard of that one before."

"Well, although the Pendle witches were most likely around before our young lady sadly lost her life, the tradition of burying animals in walls is still being exercised today believe it or not. Therefore, such practice happening in this here house is most definitely possible. Even long after the witch trials had their day, a cat was actually found in one of the Pendle cottages which was pinpointed to have been placed there much later in the eighteen-hundreds."

"Fascinating stuff," said an attentive Cain with genuine interest.

"Similar discoveries have been found in Devon and Cornwall. The thing is, escalating such a practice to include a human sacrifice is very chilling and rare. Human sacrifices are certainly not unheard of but they are very seldom documented in the tales of long ago."

"Bloody hell, this is scary shit."

"Can you remember anything else about the skeleton, Cain? Were there any objects or anything buried with her?"

Cain searched his brain for a moment, his hazel eyes shifting upwards to the right. "No sorry mate, not that I can recall. But to be honest with you, I didn't hang around to take a second look. You'll have to track down the people who took the remains away. They were messing about here for hours. We had to close the site down for a good while."

"Ok, thanks Cain. You've been very helpful. I'm really grateful for your time, but just before I let you get back to work can I show you a photograph of a young girl who is missing."

CHAPTER 9
TELL ME WHAT YOU SEE

"Dr Keeley, thank you for agreeing to meet me," said Judd shaking the woman's hand. Dr Harriet Keeley was the Head of Genetic Analysis at the University of Leicester. She was the perfect person for Judd to speak to next about the discovered remains, for it was Dr Keeley who had headed up the team that had identified the bones of King Richard III.

The King had remarkably been discovered in a city of Leicester car park in 2012, many centuries after its unknown burial. The incredible find caused a considerable amount of global attention and produced a distinct spike in English historical interest.

Now, Dr Keeley had agreed to work on the skeleton that had been found in Great Barr Hall.

"It's a pleasure, Mr Stone. Please follow me."

Dr Keeley led Judd into a nearby forensics room. He knew he was going to see a skeleton today but nevertheless he was still slightly taken aback when the collection of bones quickly appeared upon his line of sight as he walked through the door.

"So that's her?"

"That's her. The skeleton that was discovered in Great Barr Hall. I doubt she'll attract the interest of a Plantagenet King, but nevertheless the timing of her death is very interesting in a historical sense. Even though the police aren't interested in what happened to her we still feel a sense of duty to try and tell her story so that she can somehow rest in peace."

"So, have you been able to establish anything of interest yet?" enquired Judd.

"It's still early days in our assessment, but yes we have already discovered some very interesting facts about these bones. Come, let me show you."

Dr Keeley guided Judd closer to the bones.

"I wasn't expecting hair to be on the skull," said Judd.

"Hair contains keratin but no water, therefore it doesn't decompose in the same way as flesh does. Do you share your bathroom with a lady, Mr Stone?"

Judd felt his stomach churn as he thought of Brooke lying in her hospital bed with all of those tubes coming out of her, but he decided not to elaborate in the circumstances for Dr Keeley's benefit. "Err, yes I do."

"No doubt then you've felt consistent frustration at the amount of hair that becomes trapped in the plug hole of the shower? Human hair is a resilient little bugger and it's not something even the Grim Reaper can claim."

"I see. I expected a smell too."

"Not from a skeleton, Mr Stone. Once the flesh and organs have decomposed there is no real scent, but believe me rotting flesh is not something that you would want to smell."

"Actually Doctor, unfortunately from past experience in my line of work I do know what the smell of rotting flesh is like. You're right though, it's definitely not pleasant."

"It certainly isn't. Anyway, Mr Stone, I'd like to show you these unusual markings in the cheek bones." Dr

Keeley nonchalantly lifted the skull and rotated it until the light could reveal some definite incisions on the bone.

"Is that unusual?" asked Judd.

"Well this is the type of marking usually caused by an animal. The markings as you can see are in the shape of a 'V' and such markings are very consistent with a dog bite or even bites from a wild animal, perhaps. There are similar markings on the ribs too."

"So, you think she could have been killed by an animal?" asked Judd.

Dr Keeley carefully replaced the skull before answering. "When bodies are left in the outdoors they are often scavenged upon by any number of animals in the vicinity, not a pleasant thought I know, but a fact nonetheless. However, this young lady was found concealed in the construction of a building as I understand, therefore scavengers would have been unable to reach her. So, in conclusion Mr Stone, yes, it is possible that she was killed by an animal, even perhaps a domestic dog. What is curious is why she became buried in the walls of an old house after her killing?"

"Perhaps it was to hide the fact that a loving family dog could have done such a thing?"

"Possibly, although history tells us that our English ancestors weren't quite the animal lovers that we are today. This makes me doubt that someone would have covered the actions of an animal in order to save that animal's skin, so to speak. Surely if a dog had done this it would have been in a state beyond control anyway and no doubt would have needed destroying? I'm convinced that there would have been no hesitation by the owners in such circumstances. It's all very strange and puzzling at the moment."

"I once read that a dog ate part of its dead owner who had died from natural causes, but because it had been locked in the flat with them for several weeks undiscovered it simply needed to eat to survive."

"It's happened more than once, Mr Stone. I have worked on such cases, myself. Another theory could be that our victim here had been an alcoholic and fell into a deep sleep or even slipped into a coma for some reason. Believe it or not the most loving of dogs will bite their owners in an attempt to arouse them. Perhaps the dog even did this on discovering the dead body and then our deceased victim was buried in the walls after the dog's intervention?"

"So, let me get this clear in my head if you don't mind Doctor. It is possible that the dog could have simply been exposed to the freshly killed body and then it sunk its teeth into it before being shooed away?"

"Yes."

"And then our killer went on to continue the deception by placing the body in the wall?"

"It's possible."

"Oh boy."

"We should recognise that in some rare cases a dog will turn on its owner to establish his or her hierarchical position but that brings us back to the question of what human at that time would take the time and effort to cover the actions of a dog?"

Judd searched his brain as he stared at the skull which no longer held one.

Then he had an outlandish realisation and wondered if he should dare to share it with Dr Keeley. He decided at this stage he wouldn't for fear of being ridiculed.

He understood that the discovery of the skeleton had already cast a cloud over the reputation of the Lunar Society and now his imagination began to build on that cloud.

Often, conspiracy theorists suggest that a gathering of brilliant minds must be linked in parallel to something far more sinister, such as a Satanic cult or the Illuminati.

Judd was finding it difficult to suppress his excitement as the cogs of his mind whirred.

Illuminati – born out of the era of enlightenment and now widely believed (albeit secretly) to control the media, political system and even the entertainment business.

The Lunar Society – so called because they followed the light of the full moon due to the absence of street lighting at that time.

Was there a connection between these two camps?

But Judd was even more enthusiastic as he thought about another potentially incredible and bizarre twist in the discovery of this skeleton at Great Barr Hall.

The bones of the victim had bite marks upon them presenting the likelihood that a dog-like beast had played a part in the killing. And it was quite possible that the savage attack may well have been executed under the light of a full moon. The killing had certainly seemed to have occurred on Lunar Society territory.

Therefore, could it be possible that this attack had been the work of a Werewolf?

CHAPTER 10
TOMORROW NEVER KNOWS

"I'm sorry, Mr Stone. There's still no change, but she is stable."

"Only because she's on a fucking life support machine," snapped Judd.

The nurse looked hurt.

"I'm sorry, forgive me. I know that you are all doing your best."

"It's ok, Mr Stone. It can't be easy for you. Remember though Brooke is one of us so we will fight tooth and nail to save her."

"I know. I'm venting at myself really. I just feel so fucking helpless." Judd lifted Brooke's right hand and planted a kiss on her soft skin. "Does she even know I'm here? Can she hear me?"

The nurse smiled. "She can hear you. All available research points to patients in this position definitely benefitting from having their loved ones close to them and offering them touch and speech."

Judd wiped a tear from his eye. "Thank you, you're very kind. Brooke would love you to be on her ward, you know when she's back working. I'm sure she'd like you."

"Maybe one day we will work together, Brooke and I."

Judd kissed Brooke's hand once more, taking care not to disturb the tubes and sterile dressings upon his poorly wife. "I don't want to leave her just yet."

"There's no rush, Mr Stone. You take your time, but you should really get some rest yourself, you know. We'll call you if there is any change and I know you'll be back here tomorrow. You have to look after yourself as well."

"I'll just give it another hour…or two."

"I wasn't sure you'd come?" said Vina.

"I nearly didn't, but if it helps me to find your cousin then it's cool. I need a distraction anyway."

"Remember it's not just about finding my cousin, Judd. I want to know who that body was in Great Barr Hall and if it could have been me, somehow."

Judd was slightly taken aback at Vina's sharpness in tone. "Yeah, sure. I'm here for all of it, Vina."

"That's ok then."

"Anyway, we had better knock on the door," said Judd. "It's a bit chilly out here and I wouldn't want you to be late for your appointment."

Judd had agreed to meet Vina directly outside the address of her past life regression therapist. After a speedy bit of research, Judd had discovered that it seemed that a lot of hypnosis related therapists chose to trade from their home.

As they walked up the pathway of the typical Victorian property in Moseley, Birmingham, Judd quickly wondered if pop star Phoenix Easter had ever walked down this street and past this very house. Judd knew that Phoenix had grown up in Moseley.

Once again he found himself reminiscing about the enviable but pressurised job of a lifetime when he had been the bodyguard of a sweet yet troubled young lady who became a member of the notorious 27 club, joining the likes of Jim Morrison, Janis Joplin, Jimi Hendrix, Kurt Cobain and Amy Winehouse – who had all left their *then* respective lives at the tender age of just twenty-seven.

The door to the property had been immaculately painted in glossy black and still hosted its original stained-glass windows. Vina rang the bell which seemed to chime with authority and Judd could see a distorted figure emerge through the ripple effect of the frosted window. On answering the door, Judd was surprised to see a familiar face.

"Hello Vina, hello Judd. Do you two know each other or have you just met by coincidence on the pathway?"

Judd and Vina just looked at one another.

The occupant continued. "Have you come to ask me about something, Judd?" Sandy was keen to balance her understanding for Judd's presence with any duty she had in keeping his gambling addiction confidential.

"Forget me and him, do you two know each other?" asked Vina.

"Sandy, err helps me out with a slight problem I have," answered Judd.

"A problem?"

"I gamble a bit too much."

"Oh, I see," said Vina. "Sandy is my Past Life Regression Therapist."

"Yeah, I figured. She's a proper little do-gooder ain't she."

"I'll take that as a compliment, thank you Judd."

"No offence, Sandy."

"None taken."

"Vina wondered if it would be ok for me to kind of sit in and observe the regression today. In truth I'm also trying to help her but in a slightly different way to you."

"Well, it's not normal practice but if that's what Vina wants?" said Sandy turning her focus towards Vina.

Vina nodded. "Yes, please Sandy. I've hired Judd to help me with something. He's a private detective."

"And no longer a man of mystery it would seem. Well you had both better come in, I've got the room set up for you, Vina."

"Thank you," said Vina.

"Yeah, cheers," said Judd.

Once they were all inside, Sandy closed the door and led Vina and Judd down the quarry-tiled hallway to a room at the rear of the house. The room wasn't overly decorated but in spite of its relative bareness it still had a welcoming charm.

"You've lit a few candles, I see," observed Judd.

"They help to relax the client, Judd. However, you will notice the candles are fragrance free so not to confuse any memories," explained Sandy.

"Memories?"

"That's what past life regression is. A form of soothing hypnosis which takes a person back to memories from a previous life. The memories are mainly visual in the mind's eye, but can come in the form of other senses such as smells or feelings."

"Interesting stuff," said Judd.

"Now Vina, if you could please sit on the reclining chair as you usually do and make yourself as comfortable as possible, and Judd can I ask you to sit on the armchair over there out of harm's way," Sandy smiled as she instructed her house guests, always eager not to cause offence. "And Judd, can I please ask you not to attempt to communicate with Vina during the regression process. It's very important. This can only work if I'm in complete control."

"Sure thing. Understood, Sandy," assured Judd as he and Vina took their seats.

"Ok then, we shall begin. Vina, please close your eyes and relax."

The first ten minutes or so passed unremarkably as Sandy guided Vina through meadows, mountains, oceans, valleys and blue skies in order to relax every muscle of her being. Judd evaluated that this process must have been necessary to place Vina in a correct state of mind to explore her memories. Judd observed how Vina's breathing had considerably slowed down and he almost felt like dropping off himself, Sandy's voice was so soothing.

Then the journey into memories began. Judd was surprised to learn how this started with Vina recalling things that had happened only yesterday. She had practiced her cello for three hours, before heading off for a work-out in the gym followed by a one-hundred-length swim.

Sandy used a technique where she explained to Vina that she would be descending a staircase of thirty-one steps, each one representing a year of her life to date. Occasionally Vina would be asked to stop at a step and convey her memories for that age. Permission was sought by Sandy to do this, and Vina would have to agree that this could happen. Before long the memories of playing the cello were happening when Vina was a child amongst the smell of olive groves and orange trees in Spain. Vina drifted in and out of speaking in Spanish at this stage so Judd couldn't always follow what was happening. This all occurred at step ten.

"I'm going to count backwards from five, Vina, and at the final count you will be in your mother's womb and I'd like you to share with me your experiences of being in your mother's womb."

Wow, can that really happen? thought Judd.

"5-4-3-2-1, please tell me what is happening, Vina?"

"I feel safe, so very safe yet I have an intensive burning sensation throughout my tiny body. I want to be born; I want to enter this world."

"Ok that's good, Vina. The urgency could be a strong will to escape a previous life or your karmic journey has evolved to such a state that you can make a significant contribution in this, your current life. Let's not dwell here, I'm going to guide you to a door. You can open this door and walk through it to a previous life. Are you comfortable with this, Vina?"

"Si." Judd noticed how Vina was in a semi-comatose state, her eyes were closed and she was clearly oblivious of his presence and the room in Sandy's house, yet at the same time she was having a coherent conversation with Sandy whilst being in this state of detachment.

"Please walk through the door Vina, and tell me what you experience."

"I am passing through the arched doorway to the large house."

"Is it the same doorway and house that we have spoken about before, Vina?"

"Si, it is the same house."

"Please carry on, Vina."

"There is a full moon tonight. I am in the presence of a gathering of men who are sharply-dressed and jovial. They are exchanging conversation that dances between deep intellect and light-heartedness, yet I struggle to engage in the conversation. I feel almost like I don't belong there, like I'm an imposter.

"I sense that women are also present tonight but I could be confusing myself because I know that women are responsible for the cooking that is taking place. I can smell meat and vegetables. The cooking of flesh is very attractive yet I find myself running outside of the house, away from the conversation that I have no part to play in. I don't think my absence is noticed. I am drawn to the full moon. My body is starting to hurt all over. My muscles and bones are in increasing agony and they begin to feel not of my own. It feels like I'm suddenly in a different body, but the moon remains my only focus. I've come outside yet I feel claustrophobic. I'm struggling to breathe.

"Now I'm starting to feel vicious and angry. Why am I being left out of the conversation? Why don't I belong? Why am I being ignored? I won't stand for it. I refuse to be treated this way. I will be noticed. I will be noticed…"

Then suddenly both Judd and even Sandy were taken aback as they were not prepared for what happened next.

Vina began to howl!

CHAPTER 11
TURN BACK TIME

And so, ended another session at Fighting Gambling Together.

"Does anyone fancy a beer?" asked Errol, a friendly soul who Judd had warmed to over the few weeks that he'd been attending the group. Errol had spoken openly about the tales of woe that had driven him to gambling and Judd had found that he really felt for the guy. Errol had certainly experienced a rough time over the years but fortunately it seemed that nothing could ever fade his winning smile.

"As long as you keep away from the fruit machines," stated Sandy.

Errol promptly clicked his heels and saluted. "Scout's honour, Miss."

"Were you ever in the Scouts?"

"No, Miss."

Sandy couldn't help but smile. "Get out of here, you daft beggar. I'll see you next time." Everyone liked Errol, but then again, the incredibly caring Sandy seemed to like everyone.

"I'll have a pint with you mate," said Judd.

"Nice one, Judd. Anyone else care to join us?" pressed Errol.

"Yeah count me in too," said Slim. Slim was the skinny guy with the quiff who Judd had sat next to at his first meeting. Judd didn't know if Slim was a nickname or the actual real name of the young lad, but it was certainly the name that he was happy to go by.

Actually, Judd was surprised that Slim wanted to tag along because he was usually so distant and detached. Nevertheless, Judd wasn't against getting to know the youngster a little better.

"Anyone else?" asked Errol a final time, but there were no further takers.

Errol nearly choked on his stout and then sat open-mouthed for a second. "Sandy can take people back in time?"

"Yeah, kind of, but you make it sound so weird, Errol and it really isn't. It's called past life regression. There's no magic time-machine or anything. It's a proper thing, it's just a form of hypnotism, I guess, that takes you on a journey back to your previous lives," explained Judd. "I'd say it's a lot weirder that you never remove that beanie hat of yours, Errol."

"But who's to say we have previous lives? Sounds more like a load of mumbo-jumbo to me. This is our only life as far as I'm concerned. You get one shot at it mate and that's it.?"

"It's a fair point pal, but I have to say, that on the evidence I've seen it's pretty hard to doubt that genuine connections are not being made into the past."

Then Slim piped up, appearing more animated than Judd had ever seen him before. "I think you're being a bit cynical, Errol. If we only had one life to live then why would we all be gambling addicts whilst other people live in castles and palaces? That just wouldn't be fair would it?"

"Life ain't fair, Bro," said Errol, before taking another swig of his stout.

"This one maybe, Errol. But I'm telling ya, we live many different lives and learn something from each one of them until we reach our ultimate perfect balance," said Slim before turning his attention to Judd. "I love all this kind of stuff, mate. Come on, tell me what you have seen then."

Judd realised that the beer had perhaps loosened his lips a little too much and he became mindful not to break any confidentiality on behalf of Vina.

"Well, I don't really want to go too deeply into things during a quiet drink in the pub, but I have witnessed someone being taken back to a previous life as long ago as the late eighteenth-century. I must admit it got a bit weird towards the end of the session and it looked like the regression might have even shown that the person used to be a dog."

"A dog! I think I'd rather not know," said Errol.

"Oh, I would. I'd love to have a go," said Slim. "Do you think Sandy would do a past life regression on me?"

"I don't see why not," answered Judd. "You'd have to pay her of course."

"Have you ever had it done, Judd?" asked Errol.

"No, I'm way too chicken. For me what's in the past is there for a reason."

"No way man, I'd love to know about all my past lives," said Slim. "Will you guys come with me though? Just for some moral support."

Judd and Errol looked at one another and shrugged. "Yeah, sure," answered Judd for both of them. "You know how to contact Sandy, just set a session up and we will come along. But for now, Slim, in this life it's your round, so go and get 'em in."

"I'll drink to that," said Errol.

"Gentlemen, it will be a pleasure."

"And try something a bit more adventurous than cola

this time, Slim," said Judd, as the young man began to stand from his seat.

"Nah, can't stand the taste of beer. Gambling's my only vice. Same again for you two pissheads, though I presume?"

CHAPTER 12
REVOLUTION

Judd and Errol looked on with interest as Sandy took Slim back through the yesteryears using the same process that she had done with Vina.

During his past life regression, some of Slim's revelations confirmed what he had already discussed previously in the FIGHT group.

As a troubled teenager, he had taken himself away from his quarrelling parents and would lose himself in various computer games to shut out the painful noise. Unfortunately, this had been the gateway for Slim to indulge in online gambling and before he knew it, he had become hooked on the buzz he felt when entering this escapist world.

There was nothing remarkable to report from his time in his mother's womb, or on the day he was born, but then things did become a lot more interesting.

"What is the date, Slim?" enquired Sandy.

"Twelfth of June, 1796."

Straight away, Judd noticed the date linked to the same period that Vina had regressed to.

"And where are you, Slim?"

"I live in Northumberland, these days."

"These days? Where *was* home before then, Slim?"

"Birmingham. London too for a short time. I had to leave though. Forced to leave actually. Too many narrow-minded people just didn't understand so I had to move away."

"So, you fled up north?" asked Sandy.

"I fled the country."

"I'm confused, Slim. I thought you said you went to Northumberland from Birmingham."

"I did. Northumberland, Pennsylvania."

"Ahh, Pennsylvania. Northumberland, USA."

"Correct."

"Is today, the twelfth of June, a special day for some reason in Pennsylvania?"

"Very. I've been listened to here. They're going to set up the church and it's all because they respect my advice. They know what I've told them makes sense."

"A church? Why is that special, Slim? Are there not churches in USA already?"

"Not like this one. This is a unitarian church."

"Unitarian? Forgive me I may be a little ignorant regarding what that means. Can you explain a little more about that, Slim?"

"Only if you are willing to listen."

"Oh, I am. I promise you. I am very interested in what you have to tell me."

"Very well. First of all, you must note that I'm a very religious man, God is not the issue here. I believe in God wholeheartedly, but there can only be one God and that form cannot be incarnated on earth. It's ridiculous to suggest otherwise."

"Is it the Christian God you speak of or another God?"

"I speak of the same God, but Jesus was not his son. He was a man who was greatly inspired by God, I accept that. He spread the word of God extremely well, extremely well indeed, and we all owe Jesus Christ a lot but he was still only a man. He was mortal. God himself is a single entity. This belief of the Son, the Father and the Holy Ghost is simply incorrect. There can only be one God and that is the end of the matter."

"I can see how your beliefs could have caused controversy, is this why you had to leave England?"

Slim looked visibly distressed as he reflected on the question. "They burned my house down."

"Who did, Slim?"

"My name wasn't Slim. The name of my family was ingrained on that house and they burned it down to the ground. It was my family home."

"Are you able to tell me your name in this life, Slim?"

"My name is Joseph. Joseph Priestley and it was the Priestley House that those bastards burned to the ground. It had been the most impressive house in Sparkbrook. After all I had done for the people of Birmingham too, this is how I was repaid. That stirrer Pitt put them up to it."

"Pitt?"

"William Pitt."

"Pitt the younger?" asked a slightly startled Sandy.

"That's him."

The name William Pitt the younger resonated with everyone in the room, even if they lacked the detailed historic knowledge of the youngest ever British prime minister, he was a name familiar to most people.

"And your name is Joseph Priestley?"

"It is. I already told you that, didn't I?"

"You did, forgive me. I just want to be sure of the facts here because what you are telling me is truly fascinating."

"Very well."

"It must have been awful for you, Joseph. To lose your family home that way. Do you have friends in America? Are you happy there now?"

"I would have been happier if I hadn't been driven out

of my own country, but yes I have friends here. Benjamin and Thomas in particular. They're nearly as clever as me," Slim managed a wry smile. "Although I have to say that James was a good friend too. I'm sorry that I had to leave him behind in England, amongst others."

"James?"

"James Watt. He's a good man."

The name of Joseph Priestley had rung some kind of bell with Judd. It was a name he was sure he must have heard before although he was ignorant to its significance, if any. At the point of hearing the name James Watt however, Judd couldn't help himself and he blurted out a question: "Are you a member of the Lunar Society?"

Sandy shot Judd an uncharacteristic angry stare, making Judd mouth the word 'sorry.' Fortunately, Judd's intervention hadn't railroaded the session and Slim provided an answer.

"Yes, I am a member of the Lunar Society."

"Thank you, Joseph," said Sandy, relieved Slim was holding his hypnotic state. "We know that The Lunar Society were a very talented and clever group of individuals. Please, remind us of what your contribution was, Joseph. You mentioned that you had done a lot for the people of Birmingham."

"In actual fact, I have done a lot for the world in general. For example, I publicly supported the French upheaval, I wrote about it too. I was prepared to put my name in writing to support the cause."

"Are you referring to The French Revolution, Joseph?" enquired Sandy.

"Yes I am. It didn't make me very popular with everyone and not everyone agreed with me but overthrowing the monarchy was the right thing to do in France."

"Did you contribute anything else to the world, Joseph?"

"You could say that. I'm passionate about making the

world a better place. Especially where religion and politics are concerned. Some judge me as being a bit of a rebel and a troublemaker but it's important that people are properly educated on religion and politics. Only education can enable people to see things for what they really are. Anyway, apart from all that I happened to discover a little thing called oxygen, which just happens to keep us all alive."

"Really? That's remarkable."

"There's a relationship with plants and trees too you know." Slim began to get more passionate in his speech, just as he had done in the pub when talking about the concept of past life regression. "Don't you find it amazing how the rays of the sun, the air that we breathe and all the various other gases such as carbon dioxide play such a huge part in our existence, yet not one of them can be seen by the naked eye?"

"I've never really thought of things like that before but yes, it is amazing. I guess we take their presence for granted."

"Well, I have spent a lot of time understanding how these gases affect us."

"It seems that we certainly owe you a lot, Joseph."

"You flatter me, I simply discovered their existence. It is God who has created these gases for us. However, through my experiments I have been able to manipulate these gases in order to enhance our palate."

Sandy frowned. "Our palate? I'm intrigued, do go on Joseph."

"It sounds absurd, but I have been able to make bubbles appear in every day drinks. I have changed their consistency in order to expand our repertoire of potable liquids."

'So, what you are telling me is, is that you have invented fizzy drinks too Joseph?"

Errol turned to Judd and whispered something to him. "Well that certainly explains things, mate. Now we know what accounts for his love of cola."

CHAPTER 13
SUSPICIOUS MINDS

The revelations of Slim's past life regression prompted Judd to research Joseph Priestley further. Priestley had been a Yorkshireman but Judd was pleasantly interested to find that following his discovery of oxygen much of Priestley's other ground-breaking work had been accomplished in Birmingham.

Judd also discovered that everything that had been articulated during the regression was validated in the historical works of non-fiction. Not surprisingly, it turned out that Priestley had been a controversial figure who openly supported the French Revolution and the dismissal of the Christian belief of the Trinity. Priestley stated that it was incorrect to view God as three entities: The Father, the Son and the Holy Ghost. He believed that Jesus had not been an incarnate of God but rather a saviour who had spread the word of God.

Unfortunately, his beliefs had led to the 'Priestley Riots' which had largely centered on the attack of his family home in Sparkbrook known as 'Fairhill'. Nevertheless, once Priestley had fled to America, he founded the

Unitarian church based on the beliefs that he had held so passionately.

It had been unfortunate that Priestley had felt the need to bid farewell to his good friends of the Lunar Society, of which he had undoubtedly been a prominent member. However, the company that he then went on to keep in America turned out to be just as prestigious as the men he had left behind.

Priestley's American companions included the likes of Benjamin Franklin and Thomas Jefferson no less. Franklin had been a pioneer of electricity and had conducted the famous kite and storm experiment, whilst Jefferson had just happened to have become the third president of the United States.

Judd found it comical, in a way, that Slim, this skinny and unassuming computer game enthusiast had once been Joseph Priestley. Priestley had been a charismatic outspoken theologian, chemist, political theorist and philosopher driven by his own controversial theories.

A picture of Priestley also showed his hair to be combed flat against his skull, which was quite a contrast to Slim's dancing quiff.

Judd concluded that reincarnation could serve to maintain characteristics and recognisable threads throughout the progression of lives. However, he also recognised that it sought to provide a number of differing experiences in order to achieve a balanced journey of evolving existences that are encountered by any given individual.

Inevitably, Judd went on to discover a great deal more information about the other members of the Lunar Society as well as Priestley.

Like most people he had already been aware of the existence of James Watt, the legendary Scotsman who had developed the steam engines that had enabled mass production in the factories during the Industrial Revolution.

Judd was no stranger to Watt's friend either, the Brummie Matthew Boulton, a leading industrialist who had also ensured the introduction of an Assay office in Birmingham.

Being a Brummie himself, Judd had been familiar with the concept of the Lunar Society for quite some time including their presence in and around Birmingham. However, Judd having always been a less-than-interested scholar, hadn't been so familiar with their wider membership beyond Boulton and Watt or the society's full list of achievements.

Now, the more he researched them the more he became impressed with their innovative triumphs in manufacturing, botany and pioneering theories. However, it was also their admirable philanthropy that had caught Judd's attention too.

It was the Lunar Society that had been responsible for producing affordable soap and tableware that became available to the masses. It became a possibility even in the poorest households of Britain to eat meals with cleaner hands, with the food placed upon much more appealing decorative plates than previously. It seemed that the primary efforts of the Lunar Society had been made in order to achieve a better existence for all.

Nevertheless, despite their force for good, there was something that kept nagging at Judd when he once again found himself thinking about Joseph Priestley in particular. Or rather, when thinking about Priestley this in turn ignited his brain to think about the human remains that had been discovered in Great Barr Hall.

It was accepted, just as the story goes, that Priestley had been forced to flee Britain and head across the pond to the good old U S of A because of the extreme reaction to his theological and political opinions. However, wouldn't that have also been a convenient act for someone who had needed to flee the scene of a murder?

The concept messed and messed with Judd's head.

Could Joseph Priestley have been responsible for the murder of the girl discovered in Great Barr Hall?

CHAPTER 14
COME TOGETHER

Once Slim had informed the rest of the support group of his experience with past life regression, the FIGHT meeting was in danger of transforming into a spiritual debate. That was until Sandy showed an uncharacteristic level of assertiveness to get the meeting back on track.

However, the interest and curiosity surrounding Slim's tale and its ability to open most of the minds of those present became so intense, the subject soon inevitably surfaced again.

"Do you think that if we were all to undergo past life regressions it would help us to understand why we all gamble in this life, Sandy?" asked Skye, the youngest member of FIGHT.

"Possibly, but there are no guarantees. Each and every one of you have a far better chance of addressing your gambling issues by engaging in this mutual gathering here and now for the purposes that it was originally designed for," replied Sandy, trying to get back to her smiley self.

"Of course, it is," said a FIGHT member called Kingsley. Kingsley stood at six feet five inches tall and was in good physical shape, however he had a chubby baby face that belied his toned physique. "Going back in time to look at previous lives is just a load of old bollocks."

"It is not, you philistine. Open your closed little mind," retorted Skye.

"Yeah, are you saying I'm lying then Kingsley?" joined in Slim. Slim was certainly coming out of his shell more and more since his own experience.

"No, I'm not saying that, Slim. Take a chill pill, dude," said Kingsley calmly. "But when Sandy hypnotises you, you may just be relaying dreams you've had or stuff you've read or watched on TV that are buried deep in your subconscious."

"Now that's bollocks," said Slim.

"Slim, Kingsley is entitled to his opinion," said Sandy. "Listen, folks. This is meant to be a therapy session for addicted gamblers, but I can sense that curiosity is getting the better of you all. If I was willing to provide a ten percent discount for anyone in this room who wishes to undergo a regression at another time, can we all get on today with the matter at hand?"

The group looked at one another and the individuals either nodded or verbally agreed.

"Good. Thank you," said a slightly relieved Sandy, not actually expecting in reality that many would take her up on her offer when it came down to it. She was also determined that a serious conversation around the essence of past life regression would have to unfold before she agreed to put any of them under. Regression couldn't just be performed like some kind of novelty trick.

Sandy turned to Judd, determined to reignite the gambling therapy session. "Now then, Judd. Are you happy to go next? How have you been coping with any recent temptation to gamble?"

Over the next few weeks, the FIGHT group began to bond more and more. The trips to the pub that had once only been undertaken by Judd, Slim and Errol were now becoming just as inclusive for the rest of the group as the therapy sessions themselves. The only problem with this ever-increasing social arrangement was trying to keep Slim away from the pub's fruit machines.

Within the margins of the FIGHT meetings, the evolving and passionate sharing of past life regressions was bringing the group together probably even more than the moral support they provided to one another regarding their respective gambling addictions. And Judd was beginning to sense an emerging and definite theme.

Each and every one of the group's past life regressions had been somewhat remarkable. And provided a distinct insight of relevance.

They dearly enjoyed talking about their experiences with one another. Especially if they were in the pub like they were today.

Maureen, the lady with the wonky-glasses on her face discovered that in a previous life she had once lived in Stoke-On-Trent.

As a child in that particular incarnation, Maureen had suffered a severe rash which had turned into very nasty bumps filled with fluid.

When she had sat in the chair of Sandy's regression room, undergoing her trance-like experience, the feeling of sickness had become overwhelming for Maureen. As the regression continued, it actually transpired that she had been extremely lucky, considering the time period, to have survived smallpox. However, she had been left with a weak knee and a limp ever since.

The strangest thing was, even nowadays Maureen walked with a limp and had always had what she termed as 'dodgy knees'. In response, Judd had often playfully teased her by singing the football chant 'Ooh ahh, Paul McGrath'.

McGrath had been a famous footballer who, unlike his team-mates, had been unable to train during the week due to his own 'dodgy-knees'. Nevertheless, the likeable cult-hero would incredibly turn up on a Saturday and be able to perform as one of the most solid and world-class defenders of his era.

In her current existence, Maureen also had a love of pottery, especially the chalky-touch of Wedgwood's famous Jasperware range. It was hardly surprising then to learn that in a previous life, Maureen had indeed been none other than Josiah Wedgwood himself, the pottery entrepreneur who had been able to bring tableware to the masses and not just to the wealthy. Maureen had been blown away with this discovery.

During her regression, she had been able to describe in vivid detail Etruria Hall, the prestigious Wedgwood family home in Stoke-On-Trent. But she had also been able to refer to a couple of other impressive homes, these being two of the meeting places for the Lunar Society: Soho House and the significant Great Barr Hall. The latter of course being where the skeleton had been found by the construction worker, Cain.

Josiah Wedgwood had himself been a highly-valued member of the Lunar Society.

In contrast to Maureen's genuine desire to learn about any previous incarnations, Kingsley had decided to undergo one of Sandy's so-called past life regressions with a view to putting a stop to all of this nonsense and to prove everybody wrong.

Sandy had explained to him that without an open mind his session may not work for him, but once she had suitably relaxed him and taken him down his stairway of lives, even Kingsley's cynicism was destined to fade.

Starting with a regressive journey of his current life, Kingsley painfully relived the day of his tenth birthday party where he had tearfully watched the awful beating that his father had bestowed upon his mother.

Sandy had used all of her expertise to move Kingsley away from this hurtful episode as swiftly as had been possible.

Subsequently, Kingsley was taken as far back as the late eighteenth century where he had been able to describe the Birmingham of that period but also the East Midlands area. He also held fond memories of the charming cathedral city of Lichfield where he had lived for a time writing poetry.

However, still within this particular incarnation, the peripatetic Kingsley had also been able to speak of being educated at Cambridge and Edinburgh.

He had also been able to provide an insight into having an obvious eye for the ladies – something that was not too far removed from the Kingsley of the twenty-first century.

It had been Kingsley's countless affairs that had reached a point of unforgiving for both of his now ex-wives. The affairs had led to the breakdown of both of his marriages and in turn he had become a gambling addict.

Kingsley became a father who inevitably could not have been considered as an ideal role model for his kids, and he bitterly understood this more than anybody.

These days, he hardly saw his seven children from two different women, although he missed them dearly and would love to be more of a part of his kid's lives. Unfortunately, he had completely burnt his bridges with his two ex-partners and the loyalty of the children squarely fell on their side.

However, as Lunar Society member Erasmus Darwin, even twenty-first century Kingsley paled in comparison when it came to reproducing the human race, his past incarnation having fathered an incredible fourteen children. This also included two illegitimate daughters.

Erasmus Darwin had been a visionary, creating a theory of evolution some sixty years before his famous grandson Charles and he had been a main instigator of abolishing the slave trade – perhaps playing into Kingsley's ethos of being kind to his employees.

In spite of his philandering, Kingsley remained a very successful businessman who was a pleasure to work for.

He owned a variety of marketing ventures and when not gambling his money away, he would splash it out on his employees gaining the reputation of being a 'top boss'. He would often treat them to a drink or a meal at a pub or restaurant, and he would be especially generous with his money at the annual Christmas parties where no expense would be spared.

In the workplace he was what is often described as being a 'people person', whilst outside of work, Kingsley liked to go the pub with his mates and he obviously enjoyed the company of women.

Kingsley could be cocky, but he liked to be liked and he saw it as his duty in life to spread his love around unreservedly – but having little in the way of moral boundaries, this attitude had obviously become his downfall.

So naturally, in true Kingsley fashion, it was he who had made sure that he would next go to the bar to buy the ensuing round of drinks, indicating that he now viewed his misplaced cynicism as a trigger to make amends.

"I'll help you carry the load," offered Slim.

"Cheers, pal."

As the group waited for Kingsley and Slim to return from the bar, Judd looked about him and reflected on how this 'disease' of gambling was truly indiscriminate. This group represented many varied walks of life, yet each and every one of them were addicts. He also realised that this eclectic mix of people were in no doubt taking shape as the reincarnations of the Lunar Society.

"Errol, what do you make of these past life regressions?" enquired Judd.

"I have to say, Judd, that what we are hearing so far is very interesting. Do you think they are really experiencing past lives or just memories from reading books or something?"

Judd paused. "I don't know. I'm not really sure but they seem genuine recollections from a past life."

"Perhaps we will only know for sure if we do it too?"

"What?"

"You know, undergo a past life regression. I will if you will," said Errol.

Judd thought about it for a moment. He wasn't keen but he indulged his friend. "Yeah I guess you're right. I'll discuss it with Sandy."

Just then, Kingsley and Slim returned with the round of drinks.

"Well who is this lovely lady, can I get you a drink?" asked Kingsley.

Judd hadn't noticed Vina enter the pub even though she was standing right behind him. She looked stony-faced for some reason. "No thank you, I don't accept drinks from black men."

Kingsley could hardly believe what he had just heard. "Excuse me?" he said.

Vina moved one corner of her mouth, producing a kind of half-smile. "I'm joking."

"Err. Right, ok. Very funny," said Kingsley a bit perturbed.

An awkward silence fell across the group which Judd felt compelled to fill.

"Everyone, this is Vina, a, err friend of mine. Vina, you've just met Kingsley, this is Slim, Errol, Maureen…"

Vina interrupted Judd preventing him from introducing anyone else. "Hello, to you all" she said steely. "Judd, I need to speak with you in private."

"Can't it wait? Sit down and join in the fun."

Vina narrowed her eyes. "No, it can't wait."

"Excuse me guys and gals. I'll be back in a minute." Judd led Vina away from the crowd.

"Hashtag awkward," said Slim when he knew Judd and Vina were out of earshot.

"Mmmm, whoever that chick is her face is certainly more pretty than her social etiquette," remarked Errol.

"Perhaps, she's having a bad day," offered Kingsley,

more magnanimously than he needed to.

From afar the group observed the exchange of body language between Judd and Vina. It was clear Judd was far from comfortable.

"Did you have to be so fucking rude, back then. They are my friends," said Judd.

"Your friends look like the cast of Fraggle Rock."

"What the fuck has gotten into you, Vina?"

"Do you have any news on my cousin?"

"I'm working on it. These things take time."

"So why are you spending your time drinking in the pub with these jokers? I'm paying you good money, Judd."

"I don't like your tone, Vina. You have to trust me if you want me to find, Rosa. But if you think you can find someone better equipped than me to help you, then crack on and we'll call it a day."

Vina paused for a moment, then her mood strikingly changed. She stroked Judd's face as she spoke more softly. "Forgive me Judd, I'm just a little frustrated that's all. I know that you are the best there is to find my cousin. I'm sorry."

"Fuck me, I reckon he's in there now," said Slim as the group continued to observe.

"Shush, pipe down, Slim," said Errol. "They're coming back."

Judd and Vina soon reached the tables where the members of the group were seated.

"Kingsley, I must apologise to you. It seems my attempt at a joke somewhat backfired. May I still have that drink you were offering?"

"Sure thing. What's your poison?"

"Gin and Tonic, please." Vina was now smiling for real it seemed.

"One Gin and Tonic coming up."

CHAPTER 15
SATURDAY NIGHT'S ALRIGHT (FOR FIGHTING)

The evening came to a natural end. Maureen and a couple of others had already left the pub and the remaining associates would soon be following.

"I've really enjoyed myself this evening, it was nice to meet you all," said Vina. "Judd would you walk me to the train station, please?"

"Err, yeah of course. I'll see you guys next time, I guess."

"Not if we see you first," joked Errol. "Seriously, I'll text you, Judd."

'Ok see you soon.'

Rounds of "See ya," echoed from the vicinity of the pub where the FIGHT members had gathered.

Errol, Slim and Kingsley were seated together and they attentively watched Judd and Vina exit through the double doors to leave the building.

"Do you reckon he's on a promise tonight?" said Slim.

"Well if it were me in Judd's shoes, then I definitely wouldn't be saying no," said Kingsley. "Even though the lovely Vina and I did get off on the wrong foot. That accent of hers was so sexy."

"You wouldn't say no to anyone," remarked Slim.

"That's probably true. I must confess that my addiction is not solely restricted to gambling," replied Kingsley.

"Nah, he won't do it," said Errol.

"You reckon?" said Kingsley.

"Judd's married, you know," said Errol.

"So, what's the story with this chick if he's not going to bang her?" asked Kingsley.

"I honestly don't know. You know how cagey Judd can be, but she's got something to do with his line of work as far as I can tell," said Errol. "I doubt Judd would cheat on his missus in the circumstances."

"Circumstances. What Circumstances?" enquired Slim.

"Judd's wife is in a coma. She's in intensive care. The poor lady got shot."

"You're shitting me?" said Kingsley.

"I'm afraid not. I only wish I was."

'Shit, I didn't know that," said Slim. "That's fucking rough."

"Yep, it certainly doesn't get much worse," said Errol finishing the final dregs of his pint glass. "Come on let's hit the road and call it a night."

"It's a night," said Kingsley.

Judd and Vina were walking towards the train station when a flurry of wolf-whistles began to be aimed towards Vina from across the street.

"Just ignore them," said Judd.

"Jesus, wolf-whistles. Is it the 1980s?"

Judd glanced over to where the insolent activity had derived from. Although it was dark there was just enough streetlight to make out the figures of five individuals.

The gang were eager to get a reaction and ignoring the whistles only seemed to generate a heightened level of harassment from them. They soon made their way across the street and took up a unified shape in order to block the path of Judd and Vina.

"Let us pass," demanded Judd.

"Say please," said a stocky-built guy who had replaced his hair with tattoos. The ink served to camouflage the entire area of his shaven-head. Judd could make out a depiction of a spider's web but the rest just seemed to blur into non-descript patterns and ineligible scrawl.

"Please," said Judd through gritted teeth.

The tattoo-headed guy stepped aside, as if he was going to let them through in return for Judd complying with his request, but then he soon stretched out an arm to block the path of Judd and Vina once again.

Judd stared hard. "I said please, and I said it nicely. Now move your fucking arm before I break it in two."

"What the fuck did you just say?"

"You heard me."

"Ok, ok I'll let you pass...once you empty your pockets that is. We want your phones, your cash and your credit cards. Once we have those you can carry on with your little journey."

"No fucking way," said Judd.

"You're really starting to get on my fucking nerves," said the tattoo-headed thug, who was now firmly squaring up to Judd.

Vina attempted to defuse the situation. "Judd, come on let's just give them what they want."

"You need to listen to your girlfriend, Judd. She seems a whole lot smarter than you. She knows that if you don't give us what we want then you're going to get seriously hurt."

Then another voice that belonged to the gang joined in. This latest male didn't have any tattoos on his head but Judd noticed one on his neck. It was a picture of a bird, a swallow to be exact and that indicated that this guy had been responsible for at least one murder in his life. "I've got a better idea. Why don't we let these two lovebirds put on a bit of a show for us?" and with that he reached out and lifted Vina's dress.

Vina quickly pulled away, protecting her modesty as best she could. Her reaction generated howls of laughter from the members of the gang.

"You're disgusting," she said, but this just made them laugh even more.

"Don't you fucking touch her again," said Judd.

The laughing stopped.

"You're either very brave or very fucking stupid, mister," said the guy with the inked swallow on his neck.

Tattoo head spoke again. "We want a show and then we want your possessions. We don't mind which order you do it in but just fucking do it. Now."

Judd looked the tattooed monster straight in the eye and spoke very calmly and deliberately. "Look, we don't want any trouble. We are not giving you our possessions and we are not putting on any kind of show. Please just let us pass and we can all just let that be the end of the matter. I bid you a very pleasant rest of the evening, Gentlemen. Come on Vina, we're going."

Tattoo head pushed Judd hard in his chest. "You're going nowhere."

Vina was becoming very scared. "Please, just let us past," she said, her voice trembling with increasing fear.

Vina's plea fell on deaf ears. "You know what? I've had enough of this. Come on guys. Let's finish them."

Judd sensed what was about to happen and as the ringleader raised his fist to strike Judd, Judd simply stepped to the side and knocked his would-be attacker unconscious with a single punch to the jaw, resulting in his tattooed head striking the ground.

A shaven-headed Asian man stepped forward next, but again before a punch could land on Judd, Judd had separated his fingers, tilted his hand back and delivered a classic palm hell strike to the Asian man's nostrils. Pushing upwards Judd broke the thug's nose with ease.

Judd followed up on that manoeuvre by spinning one hundred and eighty degrees in the air and landing a spinning wheel kick to the man with the swallow tattoo. As the brute fell to the floor, Judd jumped in the air and stamped full force onto his face, claiming his second broken nose in almost as many seconds.

This left two remaining gang members for Judd to deal with and sensing the odds weren't in their favour each of them pulled out a knife.

A connection was quickly attempted as one knife was thrust towards Judd. He managed to pull away from the severity of the strike and achieved to block the blade with his forearm, which prevented it coming into contact with any of his vital organs. However, the knife still found a way to cut through his shirt and dig into him.

The other gang member attacked Judd from behind, opting for a downward thrust of his knife, which found its way into Judd's shoulder. A second attempt to knife Judd in the back didn't materialise as Judd sent a back kick into his opponent's kneecap causing him to crash to the floor in agony and inadvertently drop the knife.

With the other knife still stuck in Judd, the last remaining gang member looked extremely worried as Judd simply stared him in the eye and pulled the blade with ease from his own arm.

But what happened next neither of them could have guessed.

Vina jumped on the guy's back from behind and began to bite at his ear.

"Get off me you fucking bitch, get off me," but Vina had no plans to let go. As Vina chewed, Judd punched the guy hard in the stomach with his free hand and then followed this up with a swift kick to the ribs causing them to painfully crack.

The thug fell to the floor with the manic Vina still clinging on to his back. Eventually, she decided to pull her head up from the screaming individual and she duly spat a good chunk of his ear from her mouth.

"I'm impressed," said Judd before he buried the knife he was now holding into the leg of its owner.

Judd turned around to see that the gang member with the smashed knee cap had retrieved his knife from the floor, but he could hardly bear any weight.

Judd spoke calmly. "Do you really want to try and stick that in me again, fella?"

The guy just shook his head with both fear and resignation.

"Then hand the knife over to me, like a good boy," said Judd.

Naturally, the frightened youth complied.

"Thank you. You know, you really shouldn't play with knives, people can get hurt."

"Please, mister. Please, just leave me alone."

"Oh, I will," said Judd. "I believe that you boys have learned your lesson, albeit the hard way. But now, what to do with this knife?"

"Just take it, mister. You can keep it. Please, I beg you, just leave me alone."

"Is it a sharp knife? It seems to be. I mean it went into my shoulder easily enough. Almost like a knife through butter, some might say."

"I'm sorry," cried the desperate gang member, just about managing to retain his balance on his only useful leg. "I'm so sorry, I never meant to stab you."

'You know, a knife in the wrong hands can be lethal, but then with no hands at all it wouldn't matter would it"

"No, please."

Judd paused for a few seconds, twisting and turning the blade in his hand placing deliberate concentration upon the knife.

The thug began to whimper as Judd toyed with him.

"Oh, don't worry, what do you take me for?" said Judd. "I'm not going to chop off your hands. Anyway, this knife isn't sharp enough."

"Thank you. Thank you," the thug's sigh of relief was almost tangible.

"I'm a very reasonable man, err, actually, what is your name?"

"Dane."

"Dane, as I was saying. I'm a very reasonable man, so here's what I'm going to do. I'm just going to remove the pinky from your stabbing hand, just so you have a little and useful reminder of how careless it is to play with knives. Then I'll bury the knife into your leg just like I did with your dickhead friend over there. After all, I'm not a thief so I really should return the knife to you."

"No, please. Don't. I beg you."

"Hold this joker down for me, Vina."

Dane passed out as the blade sliced through his little finger and Vina chewed on her second ear of the night.

CHAPTER 16
SALTWATER

Vina walked into her living room carrying a tray from the kitchen. In the background, Judd could hear the sound of an electric kettle heating for what seemed to be for the second time.

"You'll have to remove your top, Judd."

"Excuse me?"

"I need to see to that arm and shoulder," said Vina as she knelt down to face Judd who was sitting forward on the sofa. "I have some boiled water and I've added some Himalayan salt. In Spain we use the ocean water to heal wounds, this is the next best thing in Birmingham I guess."

Judd removed his upper garments and Vina began to bathe his forearm.

"You should really go to a hospital for these wounds, Judd."

"Nah, I'll be fine. I trust your ancient Spanish remedy of using salt water. I don't fancy being stuck at A and E for hours on end, besides there'd be too many questions to answer about my injuries."

"You acted in self-defence, Judd. You know that."

"Even so, I can tell your nursing skills are working already so there's no need to head to a hospital."

Judd and Vina exchanged a smile.

"Tell me something Judd, where the hell did you learn to fight like that?"

"Where the hell did you learn to bite like that?"

Vina paused from bathing Judd's arm for a second. "I don't know what came over me. I was so incensed by the actions of those thugs it just seemed natural to get involved."

"You got involved, alright."

Vina replaced the cotton wool in the salted water and squeezed out the excess liquid before tending to Judd's wound once again. "So, come on how about you? My attack was instinctive and random, but you knew what you were doing out there, Judd."

"Well I learnt to be tough from an early age. A lot of my early years were spent in kids' homes until I was eventually taken in by a couple, so it was always a classic case of survival of the fittest a lot of the time. I worked hard not to end up at the bottom of the pile. I also went on to become a bit of a football hooligan back in the day, so I developed my fighting skills on and off the terraces you could say. It's not something I'm proud of now but that's how it was back then for me...ouch!"

"Sorry, I know it stings but I need to clean this wound," Vina tilted her head as she assessed the cut. She gave it one final wipe. "Actually, that will do for now regarding your arm, let me see to that shoulder."

Vina stood up and moved behind Judd to better access his shoulder. She had already quietly taken note of his fine physique, but now that she was exposed to the broadness of his naked shoulders and the shape of his lats, she was definitely beginning to view Judd Stone as an attractive man. Also, the courage that he had shown in protecting her had escalated a new-found magnetism towards him.

"I guess I was always a competent street fighter,

anyway," continued Judd as Vina stood behind him dabbing at his shoulder.

"Not all those techniques seemed to be street fighting, Judd."

"Well, when I joined the police force, of course part of my training was to be proficient in self-defence combat. The training touched on some moves from various martial arts so I learnt some techniques and stuff. Mind you, the tutor I had was a right bastard."

"How come?"

"He didn't take a shine to me at all, because of my background I think, and he knew that I'd been a footie hooligan so he liked to make an example of me. He'd always choose me to come to the front of the class to demonstrate his moves upon, but quite often he wouldn't hold back and he'd really hurt me. I'd always be the butt of his jokes too."

"Sounds like a really nice guy."

"Yeah, the best. He was a real bonafide bully, and he took great pleasure in ridiculing me. So anyway, I decided to invest in some martial arts classes of my own, outside of the force. I worked really hard; I mean really hard. I was like a man possessed; I was obsessed with my training. I was doing stuff morning, noon and night. In my lunch hour, first thing when I'd get up, last thing before I went to bed. Any free time I had really. I shot up the belts pretty quick in Taekwondo and also attended a regular Kung Fu class in Digbeth. Until I felt ready."

"Ready for what?"

"To teach that bullying piece of shit a lesson. The next time he used me as a punchbag in front of my peers I countered his moves and blocked everything he threw at me. It was nothing serious, I knew I had to be careful with witnesses around and I didn't want to get kicked off the force as soon as I'd joined it. I'd already fucked up being a professional footballer by beating the shit out of someone, but that's another story. But anyway, I stood up to him enough to send a clear message to him, and to those watching for that matter, that this wanker was never going to use me for his entertainment again. He told me to sit down and that was that, and do you know what?"

"What?"

"He never did call me up in front of the class again. But that's not the whole story."

"Go on," Vina continued to dab and cleanse Judd's shoulder wound.

"He whispered in my ear to meet him in the police gym at the end of my shift. Seems he didn't like the fact the worm had turned in front of his students and he accused me of ridiculing him. Can you believe it? After all he'd put me through. Anyway, so we met and he wanted to teach me a lesson and he proper went for me. It was a close fight but ultimately, I had to make sure that I beat that bastard. I would have happily died if it meant that I won that fight."

"What happened?"

"I broke my finger on his head but I broke his ribs too. Neither of us were gonna stop until one of us was unconscious or dead. Fortunately, it was the former. I walked out of that gym battered and bruised like I'd never been hit before, or since, but I still walked out a lot sooner than he did. I left him sleeping like a fucked-up baby and he was no doubt pissing blood for a few weeks after because I was pissing blood myself for a fortnight. I know I had broken his nose too."

"Good for you, Judd. But how did you get away with it?"

"Next lesson he acted like nothing had happened, but you could see the other colleagues looking at his bruised face, and then mine, and then back at his and they must have put two and two together but nobody was prepared to ask the question. So as far as I know it stayed our little secret but that nasty bastard never bullied me, or as far as I know, anyone else again."

"That's good."

"But you know what, it's funny how things work out and maybe I was meant to cross paths with that horrible fucker."

"How d'ya mean?"

"Maybe I owe him a lot of gratitude, because without that determination and drive to get even with that instructor I wouldn't have gotten out of half the scrapes that I've been involved in over the years. And more importantly, I would never have been able to protect you from a gang of knife wielding thugs, now would I?"

Suddenly the feeling of the damp cotton wool on Judd's shoulder turned to one of wet lips on his neck as Vina began to kiss at his skin.

"What are you doing, Vina?" asked Judd, knowing that he should pull away, make his excuses and leave.

"I'm saying, thank you," said Vina in between the kisses.

Judd had to concede that Vina's hot lips felt good. Her technique in kissing his neck, and now reaching forward and stroking his torso delicately with her hands, seemed as impressive as his had been in breaking the bones of the gang members.

Judd closed his eyes and succumbed to the touch of a beautiful woman, forcing another one: his wife, Brooke, from his thoughts.

After placing Judd in a near-trance, Vina gently pushed him down into a horizontal position on the sofa and climbed on top of him.

They kissed and touched one another with a strong passion, strangely ignited by the violent encounter they had experienced together earlier that night. It seemed to provide a bond between them that only they could understand.

They fell onto the floor with Judd now positioned on top of Vina.

Vina broke her mouth away from Judd's to access some air, before whispering in Judd's ear with her sexy

Spanish accent. "Judd, it's time I had something other than a cello between my legs."

CHAPTER 17
I WANT TO HOLD YOUR HAND

In spite of what Vina had whispered to Judd that night as they embarked on their lovemaking, watching her perform in concert made him realise that Vina had been born to have a cello between her legs.

Judd had started to become a regular attendee at the CBSO concerts performed at Birmingham's Symphony Hall. Vina's ability to play her musical instrument was beyond impressive and watching her incredible harmonious competence unfold served to make Vina seem even more attractive to Judd.

In fact, Vina's virtuoso cello playing seemed to turn Judd on just as much as the violence that had been dispensed in defeating the thugs had served to turn Vina on. Each and every concert always seemed to be followed by a session of hot passionate sex between the explosive couple.

Judd was still a resident at the Rotunda building which was only a short walk across town from the Symphony Hall. Brooke had moved in with him since their marriage, so Judd conducted his relationship with Vina either at her apartment or a hotel room. Judd had foolishly kidded himself that by avoiding the Rotunda, the affair didn't seem as bad as it actually was.

Yet if he dared to look deep within himself, he would soon have come to realise the plain truth that he was shagging another woman while his wife lay in a hospital bed in a coma. It was a simple as that.

Anyway, Vina liked the lovemaking to unfurl at her place as she had cameras set up all around her bedroom. She liked to film her and Judd.

Vina was extremely adventurous in the bedroom, something else that drew Judd towards her. He was like a moth to a flame where the sultry Spaniard was concerned. He was weak, he knew that deep down, but the lack of resistance to temptation always seemed to be worth it as Vina was just so damn hot. And willing.

Following their latest episode of intense love making both Judd and Vina were feeling a distinct level of exhaustion and satisfaction. As they cuddled, Judd tenderly stroked Vina's naked breasts with his fingertips, making random shapes and circles on her smooth skin and around her nipples. As his fingers wandered, he soon began to fixate his touch on a reddish-coloured blemish on her left breast.

"Don't, Judd. I really hate that birthmark. What a fucking place to get one huh?"

"Are you crazy? I love it," said Judd. "It makes your tits stand out from all the others."

"Others? You get to see a lot of tits, do you?" said Vina teasingly.

"I didn't mean it like that," said Judd. "I have to assume that most breasts don't carry birthmarks. Your birthmark makes you special. It's very distinctive. Besides, it's not very big is it? It's even unusual in shape, it reminds me of an anchor." Judd reached his head forward and kissed the birthmark. "You know I once heard that birthmarks are caused by a trauma experienced in a previous life."

"Really? That's interesting."

"Yeah, apparently so. I wonder what the story of your mark is then, Vina."

"I don't know. Perhaps I had my heart broken? Probably by someone like you, Judd."

"Or perhaps you've always been this nymphomaniac in all of your previous lives and one of your kinky sex sessions got a bit out of hand."

Vina grabbed hold of the pillow from under her head and playfully hit Judd with it. "You're such a cheeky shit, Judd Stone. You be careful that I don't inflict a birthmark on you for your next life. How about a scar across your balls?"

"Err, no thanks. I think I like them just as they are."

"Well that makes two of us…for now," Vina cupped Judd's testicles in her hand. She realised that whenever a woman was in this position the power that she suddenly held was remarkable. "Make sure you never upset me, Judd Stone."

"I'll keep it in mind."

CHAPTER 18
YESTERDAY

The FIGHT meetings were becoming more and more focused on discussing past life regressions than airing the need to gamble. Even Sandy, who had been keen to keep the two things separate was beginning to recognise the value of the group's interest in finding out about their past lives. It had caused the group to bond and more importantly, and somewhat miraculously, the members had more or less stopped gambling! It was as if the past life regressions had become a platform for gambling therapy in their own right, or at the very least they had certainly become a useful distraction.

So now Sandy was more than happy to let the discussions flow, recognising that the interest had evolved far beyond playful curiosity to one of genuine shared interests.

The latest revelations had established that the football results and horse racing gambler, Kenny, had previously been the mathematician and philosopher, William Small.

In his current life, Kenny was pleased that he had made it successfully to the age of forty-five after discovering that

Small had died at the tender age of just forty of suspected malaria, his illness being diagnosed by his friend, Erasmus Darwin.

Sandy had quietly wondered if the traits of mathematicians and great minds of the past lives now somehow translated to the interest in gambling in contemporary times for the FIGHT members. The need to gamble can be born out of a strong need to occupy the mind coupled with a strive to be the best – i.e. to win! To be a serious gambler you rarely relied on luck, a great deal of analysis took place in the run up to a bet. Risks could be extreme but were often calculated.

Skye Collins, the young bingo obsessive, turned out to have been another Scottish William – William Murdoch, the inventor of gas light. It was interesting to discover the theory of a past life within a past life – Murdoch ended up living in the court of the Shah of Persia. There he was believed to have been the reincarnation of Marduk the God of light.

Abdul, who was a bit of a wide-boy, but nonetheless harmless enough, completed the set of Lunar Society Williams. As Shropshire born botanist and doctor William Withering, he had discovered the treatment of heart disease using an extract from the foxglove plant. In his current life, Abdul worked in an independent chemist store. The coincidence didn't escape anyone.

All the talk of these great-minded Williams, who had made such a telling contribution to society, naturally led Judd to think of his departed friend, William Chamberlain. Chamberlain, who had himself been in the possession of a brilliant mind, could easily have been a member of the Lunar Society.

And God only knew how much Judd missed him.

Judd became shaken from his sad thoughts when it was revealed that Abdul's friend, Aki, had previously been James Keir, the chemist responsible for making soap affordable to the masses.

Abdul and Aki were prolific visitors of the local casinos. Realising their casino life-style was getting out of hand, together they had made the decision to support one another by attending FIGHT.

The Polish carpenter, Nikodem (known as Niko) and the widowed grandmother of eight, Wanda, completed the set of Lunarticks cum FIGHT members as clockmaker John Whitehurst and inventor Richard Lovell Edgeworth respectively.

Up to this point, neither Judd nor Errol had participated in a past life regression. For Errol, the curiosity was becoming far too intense and he turned to his friend. "I'll have a go if you do, mate."

"I dunno. I'm not sure I want to know who I used to be. I prefer to let sleeping dogs lie," said Judd.

"Come on you've got to mate; it could be fun. Everyone else has had a go. Besides, it was you who kind of got them into doing all of this."

The others joined in. "Come on Judd, we should all do it.," offered Slim. "There's got to be a reason why we were all once connected so long ago and now here we are all over again. We need to find out who you are, mate."

Judd thought for a second. In truth he wasn't keen but he felt obliged to follow suit. "Ok, ok I'll do it. But only after Errol."

"Well then," said Sandy. "There's no time like the present, Errol."

Everyone moved closer to the two chairs in the centre circle, either by leaning forward attentively in their own chairs or making the effort to get up and step closer to Sandy and Errol. They waited with baited breath as their eyes transfixed on the scene.

"Actually, I hope this works with such an intense audience," said Sandy seeming a little concerned. "I usually conduct past life regressions in much more comfortable and secluded surroundings. Are you sure you want to try here and now, Errol? I don't wish you to feel pressurised into taking part. You can come over to the house another time if you prefer."

"It's fine, go for it."

"Ok, but only if you're sure, Errol."

"I'm sure."

Sandy's process to take Errol on a journey through his memories was standard. She guided Errol over meadows, mountains, oceans, valleys and blue skies in order to relax him, and just as Judd had witnessed with Vina and Slim, he noticed his friend's breathing drop pace and begin to deepen.

Sandy, then once again used the technique where she took Errol down the stairs that represented his life. His staircase had fifty-three steps to signify the years he had so far spent on earth as the likeable Errol Campbell.

Sandy sought permission from Errol to stop at his thirty-fourth step, but Sandy soon re-evaluated the situation and guided Errol down the other stairs, as most of his thirty-fourth year had seemed to have been spent in the bookies losing money on horse and dog racing.

Next came the twenty-first step, where Errol spoke fondly of his time singing lead vocal in a SKA and reggae band, except it seemed that any attempt at undertaking serious band practice had always seemed to succumb to smoking weed and drinking rum.

On his eighth step, Errol recalled how he had been shirtless in the back yard of his parent's house in Handsworth, Birmingham. He had not worn a shirt on that day because it had been one of the hot summer days of 1970's Birmingham.

His memory was so vivid that he could describe the smell of the freshly washed cotton laundry hanging on the washing line which had compromised his space for practicing keepy-up with the football. When the dirty ball struck his father's starched white shirt, his larger-than-life mother had suitably chastised him with a strict flurry of verbal discipline.

When he reluctantly had to go inside the house to eat at his mother's insistence, the fragrance he described changed to a mixture of pine and West Indian cooking caused by the cleaning products of the day and his mother's specialty of curried goat. The latter soon made him forget about playing football in the yard – his mom had been an amazing cook.

Errol had been able to paint a picture of a very happy childhood home, one filled with love in spite of the high standards of discipline – something not uncommon in a 1970s West Indian household. The wallpaper had been gaudy and the décor colour scheme had clashed with that of the second-hand three-piece suite. Much of the walls had been covered with religious pictures and an impressive collection of house plants had dominated the downstairs rooms.

Not much later, Sandy had taken Errol into the life that they had all been waiting for. He too had been able to recall being a participant of the Lunar Society – and as it turned out, he had just happened to be have been one of its most significant members.

"Please walk through the door to this previous life Errol, and tell me what you experience."

"I will meet my friends tonight for there is a full moon," Errol's accent had changed to one of a Scottish nature.

"Will you be meeting at Great Barr Hall?"

"No, not this evening. Nor at Heathfield Hall?"

"Heathfield Hall?"

"That's my home. I had it built in Handsworth. I put my considerable earnings to good use having that house built. I was inspired by the homes of my friends. They both live relatively nearby. You mentioned Great Barr Hall, that's the home of the Scott family although my friend Samuel Galton is leasing the establishment at present. Great Barr Hall has an impressive lake and I wanted the same at Heathfield Hall, whereas in the case of Matthew's home I wanted warm air pumped through the house to keep my family comfortable during the harsh winters we suffer in Birmingham. I also decided to have a nice circular driveway built."

"Who is Matthew?"

Errol began to laugh. "Who is Matthew? Why Matthew Boulton of course. Everyone knows who Matthew Boulton is in these parts. He is Birmingham's favourite son and so he should be, he's done so much for this city. Surely you have heard of him?"

"Yes, I have, and I have heard of you of course. You are James Watt are you not?"

The spectators looked at one another with amazement. Errol Campbell had once been the innovative industrialist who had developed the world beating steam engines that powered the hearts of the factories during the industrial revolution, including the vast production of tin in the mines of Cornwall.

"I am he."

"So, are you meeting at Matthew's home this evening? Soho House?"

"Yes, we meet there on most occasions, my clever friends and I. It's only a relatively short walk for me to Soho House, but I still tend to use the light of the moon as a guide to find my way. I have an easier task than Josiah Wedgewood bless him. The poor chap has to find his way from afar afield as Stoke-on-Trent."

"Why do you meet, you and your friends, James?"

"I'm sorry, I'm struggling to hear you over all of this factory noise."

"Factory noise? Which factory are you in, James?"

"I'm in the Soho Manufactory."

"You must be very proud of your steam engines, James; I was asking before what do you and your friends talk about when you meet? No doubt you speak about your steam engines?"

"Oh, I do, as does Matthew. We all tell our stories about our crazy ideas, that's why we amusingly refer to ourselves as the Lunarticks."

"That's funny, James. Tell me more about this factory you're in."

"The smell of hot metal, most of it precious, is intense but you get used to it. We turn out nice silverware but buttons and buckles too. Matthew and I aren't always here, we employ and nurture some wonderful engineering talent at the factory. It's very hot and noisy, both due to the heavy use of machinery. I don't know how Matthew puts up with the noise so close to his home but I guess as the factory's father he takes great joy and pride from it. My steam engines are driving mass production here which has pleased Matthew."

"Is Matthew there with you now?"

"No, it was not long ago that he took the short walk home."

"So, do you think the meeting with the Lunarticks tonight will be productive?"

Errol, as James Watt, smiled before answering. "Yes, I'm particularly looking forward to tonight's meeting as Josiah is bringing me a small gift in the shape of his jasperware range."

"That's very nice."

Sandy felt this to be a good point, a happy point, to bring Errol back to the here and now and within minutes the likeable character was feeling as though he was waking out of a dream. He was only slightly dazed and he could recall much of what he had experienced, astounded and privileged to have discovered that he had once been the much-admired man, James Watt.

Once satisfied that Errol was safely back in the twenty-first century, Sandy began to speak. "I'm exhausted, and time's getting on. Judd, would you mind if we undertake your regression another time?"

"Fine with me, Sandy." And it really was. Judd still

didn't want to take part.

CHAPTER 19
NOWHERE MAN

"Man, you have so got to be Matthew Boulton, dude," said Errol excitedly.

In truth, it was not only the incarnation of Matthew Boulton who needed identifying amongst this trend of Lunar Society members popping up during the FIGHT group's past life regressions. There still remained question marks over whose contemporary entity now hosted the lives of other Lunarticks such as Samuel Galton, Richard Lovell Edgeworth and John Whitehurst.

Judd thought about who in the FIGHT group these men could possibly now be assuming that connections between the two unlikely collectives were to remain as prominent. Surely even the most cynical of cynics couldn't put all of this down to coincidence.

There was himself of course – tipped as a hot favourite to be Matthew Boulton it seemed, but that still left the others unaccounted for. And who the hell had Vina once been with her vivid memories of the Lunar Society?

Of course, it wasn't compulsory that the jigsaw had to be completed by the FIGHT members but the links with the Lunar Society so far were pretty incredible.

As fascinating as all of this was, Judd realised only too well that his indulgence in the Lunar Society and his friend's past life regressions had drawn a complete blank in trying to establish a connection or any kind of a lead with Rosa's disappearance. In actual fact, he felt pretty annoyed with himself that he had lost so much ground on that particular line of enquiry, not to mention his distinct lack of investigation into finding the motorcyclist who shot him, his wife and his two close friends. The latter resulting in cold-blooded murder.

Judd decided that it was time to pull his socks up and re-evaluate his methods if he was to somehow find a way to balance the scales of justice. Somehow, he needed to fathom how this complex jigsaw puzzle really could become the bigger picture.

CHAPTER 20
I SAW HER STANDING THERE

As Judd placed the key into the door of his Rotunda apartment, he suddenly found himself in a race to answer the ringing telephone which was connected to the landline. The urgency had masked how easily the door had moved forward without the key needing to even turn - something Judd hadn't taken in.

Mr. Mustard was leaping about all over the place in order to welcome home his owner, but the dog in all his excitement was threatening to trip Judd over as he made his way to the ringing telephone.

"Hello, hello," he said slightly out of breath. He cursed the air assuming he hadn't made it to the receiver in time but then a voice replied.

"Hello, Judd."

Judd recognised the voice immediately. "Hey, Tilda. How are you?"

"Well that depends."

"On what?"

"On any progress that you've made in finding my brother's killer."

Judd squeezed his eyes shut, instantly consumed with guilt and shame. He had only recently come to realise himself that he hadn't sufficiently progressed in tracking down the killer of William and Crystal, and now his best friend's sister was bitterly reminding him of his failings. How could he have allowed himself to have become so sidetracked from finding the murderer of those so close to him, by instead focusing so intensely on the discovery of an old skeleton that in truth meant nothing to him.

But there was also a damsel in distress in the shape of Rosa Moreno, and a damsel in distress would always be his Achilles heel.

"These things take time, Tilda," said Judd trying to offer some form of justified explanation. "Ben has the force on the case and even Sab is investigating any leads overseas. A great deal of effort is being deployed on both sides of the Atlantic."

"And you are a better detective than all of those put together, Judd. William knew it, that's why he always believed in you. He was your friend; he would want you to sort this. For him and for Crystal."

Judd squeezed his eyes shut once more. "I know, I know. You're right. I'll try harder, Tilda. I promise."

Judd quickly realised that if he were to reinvigorate his focus on finding the motorcycle shooter, he would have the perfect excuse to step away from all of the pressure that he was experiencing to undertake a past life regression. He would certainly prefer to avenge his friends than to play silly buggers potentially unearthing memories that he would rather stay buried.

"I told you I'd sort it that day at the funeral, Tilda, and I meant it. I owe everything to William. You know how much I thought of him."

"I do, and him of you."

Suddenly, Judd caught sight of a blurry reflection in the glass panel of his drinks cabinet. He couldn't make out a face but he was in no doubt that there was a figure lurking behind him.

Judd's stomach flipped as he realised that he was not alone in the room.

It was at this point that it quickly registered with him how easily the door had opened during his entrance to the flat.

It had already been unlocked.

"Please be careful though, Judd," continued Tilda, oblivious to what danger was unfolding in Judd's apartment. "Like I expressed to you at the funeral, William and Crystal were obviously involved in some pretty scary stuff. I want you to crack the case and bring whoever is responsible to justice but please make sure that you don't become their next victim."

Judd stayed cool; he didn't want whoever was in his flat to know that he was on to them.

It inevitably crossed his mind just what a lousy guard dog Mr Mustard was.

Judd discreetly kept his eye on the figure behind him, but whoever it was didn't move from their position.

They seemed content to let the phone call conclude, that way there'd be no evidence for whatever they were intending to be made explicit to the caller on the line.

Judd knew that they were definitely there though. There was no uncertainty about it. They were waiting like a coiled cobra ready for their attack.

"I'll be careful, Tilda," William's sister couldn't possibly have understood just how significant those words of Judd's were at that moment in time. "I have some leads, I promise you," Judd realised that those next words were not exactly true but he was so determined to locate the killer and bring them to justice it didn't altogether feel that he was lying to Tilda. It was just a matter of time.

But first he would have to deal with the intruder in his flat.

"You do?" said Tilda.

"Yes, it's just, I wouldn't want to speak about them

over the phone if you know what I mean."

"Oh, of course. Bugged phones and all that. I know what you mean. Anyway, how's Brooke? Sorry, I should have asked after her earlier."

More guilt and shame consumed Judd.

"She…she's…not OK, to be honest with you. No worse but no better. She remains in a coma."

"I'm sorry to hear that. Stay strong Judd, she needs you."

"I know. I'll visit her later today." He meant it too. But for now, he knew that he was going to have to somehow end the call and quickly eradicate the imminent danger that he was in.

"I'll let her know that you were asking after her, Tilda. The nurses tell me it's good to talk to her and that she can hear everything."

"That's good, you do that."

Judd was ever conscious of the situation and the intruder.

"Listen, Tilda. I need a slash, I've only just got in. I'm crossing my legs as we speak. I'll call you in a couple of weeks. I promise you I'll have some news by then. We could meet up if you like."

"Ok, Judd. I'd like that anyhow. Bye for now then. Take care and love to Brooke."

"Bye."

Judd slowly placed down the receiver all the time keeping his eyes fixed on the still refection in the glass.

He was going to have to act fast. The intruder may have a gun or a knife, but unless he turned to face his assailant then he would have no hope of getting out of this alive.

In order to introduce an element of surprise and to gain some space and potential shielding, Judd threw himself to the floor, rolled in front of the settee like a commando and then stood up again ready to charge at the intruder from a preferred position of attack.

Suddenly he felt pretty silly.

"What the fuck are you doing, Judd?"

"Sab? How did you get in here?"

"You know for a private detective you really should up your security. I came in through the bathroom window."

"I live umpteen stories up!"

"I'm joking, I just couldn't resist saying that as I know it's one of your favourite Beatles songs. I used a skeleton key. I hope you don't mind."

"No, no. Not at all. It's great to see you, but you nearly gave me a heart attack."

"I'm sorry. I didn't want to interrupt you whilst you were on the phone. Mr Mustard has been keeping me company while I've been waiting for you."

Mr Mustard barked in approval and Sab ruffled the fur on the dog's head.

"Well he knows you and he likes you, so that explains why he didn't attack you. I was concerned for a moment back there that I had a pretty useless guard dog."

Sab put on a coochie coo voice as she stroked and ruffled the dog some more. "You're not useless are you Mr Mustard, no you're not. Silly old Judd."

"So why are you here, Sab? Have you quit the police department?"

"Not quite. I saw what you did there with the song, very good. Touché. But I figured that I would be more use in finding William's and Crystal's killer by helping out over here than being thousands of miles away in the States, and from what I can make out from that phone call with Tilda it seems you could do with the help so my decision was a sound one. I've managed to wangle a twelve-month sabbatical."

"But what about your research into the killing from over there?"

"Not a lot to go on I'm afraid. As yet, there are no substantial connections in the U.S to what's happened and why would there be? I've kept a couple of LAPD colleagues loosely deployed on matters but I need to be in England if I'm going to help to avenge the death of our friends."

"Well, that's wonderful. I'm really pleased to see you, Sab. I know Yasmin will be too."

"Ahh, yes. How is my little sister?"

"Forever a pain in the arse but I couldn't be without her."

"Sounds about right. Now be a good host, Judd, and go and put the kettle on. I haven't had a decent cup of tea in months."

As requested, Judd did go and put the kettle on, however the cups of tea soon inevitably became alcoholic beverages courtesy of Judd's drinks cabinet. The same cabinet with its blurry reflection that had not so long ago led him to believe that he had an intruder in his flat. The two friends laughed about that and in particular they laughed out loud about Judd's zealous reaction to undertake a commando roll across the floor.

In actual fact they laughed a lot that night, talking about old times and the fun and adventures that they had shared over the years.

The fond tales of recollection also included many that had included William, and they found themselves affectionately raising a glass to their old pal on more than one occasion.

But the mood of conversation changed when they also talked about the unsolved murder of their friend. It changed again when they went on to discuss Rosa, the missing Spanish girl.

Inevitably Judd's insecurities and guilt complex poured out to his now living closest friend. However, Sab's assessment of the situation took him completely by surprise.

"The truth is Judd, William and Crystal have gone. We can't bring them back, but this girl has her whole life ahead of her so you need to find her. You're a damn fine investigator, Judd, one of the best I've ever worked with, but you are not a super-hero. I'm here now, so you need to start sharing the load. I'll seek the justice we both so desperately want for our two friends, while you concentrate on finding that poor girl."

"Thanks, Sab, but it doesn't feel right. Tilda said William would want me to sort this."

"Really? You don't think if William was here now, he wouldn't be saying the same thing to you that I am? He would want you to find that girl, I'm sure of it. Crystal too for that matter."

Judd ran his fingers through is hair. "Maybe you're right. You know with Crystal being a medium and all, I've been looking for some kind of sign, something to point me on the right path. Some kind of a connection from her, but there's been nothing as far as I can tell."

"All the more reason to listen to me, then. I'm here, Judd, sitting right in front of you. I'm telling you that this is what you have to do. You have to find Rosa Moreno." Sab could sense the cogs of Judd's mind working away. "Look at it this way, the quicker you find the girl the quicker we can work on this thing with the motorcycle shooter together, but for now finding Rosa has to be your priority. Now go and pour me another gin and tonic."

CHAPTER 21
WAKE ME UP BEFORE YOU GO-GO

Another evening of watching Vina perform at the Birmingham Symphony Hall had been followed by an encore performance of lustful sexual aerobics in Vina's bedroom.

Having eventually fallen asleep, Judd was woken by the ringing of his mobile phone.

In order to take the call, Judd needed to disturb Vina's resting head from his bare chest, which caused her to mutter a sleepy groan of displeasure. However, her state of sleep was soon abruptly brought to an end once and for all when Judd sat bolt upright in reaction to the news he was receiving at the other end of the phone.

"What? Are you serious?... Sorry, of course you are...This is just the best news, ever."

"Yes, it's true. Mr Stone," said the voice at the end of the line.

"Well that's just amazing. Thank you for calling me. Thank you. Thank you. I'll be over right away."

Judd leapt out of bed and began to get dressed excitedly.

"What the fuck is going on, Judd?"

"I've got to go, Vina."

"Why? It's the early hours of the morning. Who the hell was on the phone at this fucking time? And why are you in such a rush?"

Judd began to tie his belt. "It's Brooke, my wife. She's woken up at the hospital. She's out of her coma."

Vina didn't exactly share Judd's excitement at his news. "So, where the fuck does that leave me?"

Judd pulled his shirt over his head. Fortunately, he had left most of the buttons done up so his haste to get dressed wasn't compromised. "Come on Vina, you knew the score. You knew that I was married."

"And so did you! Nevertheless, it was convenient for you to fuck me while your wife slept away."

"Vina, she's my wife and she has just woke from a coma. What do you expect me to do?"

"Come back to bed."

"What? You're not serious? Be reasonable."

"You be fucking reasonable. I'm not a fucking whore. I'm not your toy to pick up and use when you feel like it."

"I never said you were, Vina. Look, I'm sorry if you thought there could be anything between us on a more, err, permanent basis. That was never going to happen and I thought you knew that. I guess I should never have got involved with you like this. Not in this way."

"You are not walking out on me, Judd Stone."

"Come on Vina, grow up. We had fun but you knew how things were. My wife needs me now, surely you can understand that?"

"I understand plenty. You fucking used me."

"We used each other. We've had a good time, but now it's over. Surely you can see how things have changed?"

By this time, Judd was now putting on his shoes. He leant over to kiss Vina goodbye on the cheek. Vina pulled away.

"I'll call you. You've still hired me to find Rosa, but

that's all our relationship can be from now on. I really thought you understood the situation, Vina."

"If you walk out of that door now, Judd you will regret it."

"I really am sorry, Vina, but my wife needs me."

Judd ran out of Vina's home and straight to the hospital.

"Hey baby," said Judd taking his wife's hand. "How are you feeling?"

Brooke smiled at her husband, delighted to see his familiar face. Her eyes were sleepy but they still held that sparkle that melted Judd's heart. Her eyes had always been one of her most endearing features.

By waking from her coma, Brooke had come a long way and defied many odds, but she remained a patient in the Intensive Care Unit and was still unable to sit up without assistance.

"I'm ok, thanks. I wish you had been here when I woke up though. I was a bit confused and scared at first, I couldn't fathom where I was."

Judd became consumed by guilt and hoped Brooke couldn't read it on his face. "I'm sorry babe, I wish I had been here to watch you open those gorgeous eyes of yours. I have spent lots and lots of nights here with you, but sod's law the one night I wasn't here you go and wake up without me. I really am sorry." Judd kissed the back of Brooke's hand, careful not to disturb the tube and associated dressing.

Brooke smiled. "It's ok. You're here now."

"And always will be, Brooke. Always. This is a miracle. I'm so happy you've come back to me."

"Me too."

"I'd really like to take you home as soon as possible."

"I'd like nothing more Judd, but the doctors have told me I need to stay in ICU for a while longer. And then there's some rehabilitation to do following the damage caused by my gunshot injury. Do we know who did it yet? The shooting, I mean?"

"Not yet, but we are all working on it."

"You and William will find them, I'm sure."

Then Judd realised that Brooke wasn't aware of the tragic outcome of the attack regarding William and Crystal.

"When I said we, I meant Sab and me, babe. And maybe, Ben too. I'm afraid William and Crystal didn't make it."

The expression on Brooke's face could have painted a thousand words of sorrow. "No, not William and Crystal. Oh, Judd."

Judd consoled his wife as she cried.

CHAPTER 22
GANGSTERS

Judd figured that the quicker he could find Rosa then the quicker he could get Vina out of his life. The situation was awkward beyond comprehension, and now that Brooke had woke from the coma his guilt at betraying her was overwhelming at times.

He found that he was asking himself the same question over and over again: *How could he have done it to her?*

Judd had never stopped loving his wife all the time she had had her beautiful eyes closed with the abundance of tubes and whatnot protruding from her sleeping body. Nevertheless, Brooke's time in ICU had still conveniently presented him with the opportunity to sleep with another woman.

Judd felt ashamed of his selfish actions but he was also running scared. What if Brooke were to ever discover what he had been up to with Vina? Judd had not even considered the possibility of her finding out whilst she had been lying in a coma, the realisation which now escalated his sense of shame. By ending the affair with the cellist, he hoped that would be enough to escape such a painful discovery for Brooke, but would Vina ever settle for a simple professional relationship from a distance? Judd knew that she was a fiery one, and a tad unpredictable. All he could do was hope.

It was therefore somewhat ironic that in the withdrawal of his affair with Vina, he should turn to another of his old flames as a possible avenue for locating Rosa.

Gia Talia was one of Birmingham's most fearsome gangsters. Along with her unscrupulous brother, the somewhat warped and unhinged Ray Talia, they dominated the underworld of England's second city.

The Talias had also been on the concealed payroll of Birmingham pop star, Phoenix Easter, whilst Judd had served as her personal bodyguard, but he and they had worked in isolation rather than together during that period of Judd's life.

Nevertheless, Judd already knew Gia very well as he had enjoyed a passionate affair with her prior to his time protecting Phoenix.

Brooke had found out about their illicit relationship but had eventually been able to survive the situation and their wedding had even come after Judd's dishonest act.

Incidentally, Phoenix had sang to the married couple at the joyous occasion – a double wedding alongside William and Crystal in Las Vegas.

Gia Talia was an entirely different animal to Vina Moreno altogether. Her response had been in total contrast to Vina's when the time had come to split from Judd. Gia was sophisticated and classy, she was a woman of supreme control and her use of Judd had been equally, if not more, for her benefit than it had been for Judd's. It had very much been an affair of mutual convenience. It had served a useful purpose of enjoyment and sexual fulfilment, but it had never been a relationship that Gia Talia had not been prepared to walk away from. She would always be fond of Judd but she wasn't a woman who could ever let her emotions carry her away. After all, this was a woman who was capable of ordering extreme acts of violence or even murder if required. No man in the name of love could ever fully penetrate the harsh exterior of such a formidable woman. Nor could a man ever compromise Gia's strong sense of independence.

"Look Judd, it's like I told your friend, William. This is dangerous stuff to be getting involved in."

"What? You spoke to William? William came to see you?" Judd was surprised. Unlike himself, he had assumed that Gia Talia would have been one of the last people that William Chamberlain would have ever engaged with.

"Yes, he did come to see me. And for what it's worth I liked him. I only wish that he had heeded my warning," said Gia.

"Do you know who shot him and Crystal?" asked Judd.

"Not specifically, but he was looking in places and underneath rocks that was obviously going to lead to upsetting the wrong kind of people."

"People like you? …Sorry that come out wrong."

"If you like, or worse. Listen, Judd, what I'm about to tell you is not for common knowledge. Ok?"

"Ok."

"We almost lost the war let alone the battle."

"What do you mean?"

"The UK, including Birmingham, has been flooded with criminals from Eastern Europe. Naturally, we gave them a friendly warning about daring to muscle in on our patch, but it was only after Ray had locked their main Birmingham operator in a mystery storage container for two weeks until his kidneys began to fail that they were prepared to listen.

"We stood firm and eventually called their bluff, you know how Ray is, he would happily take on the world, but I got the impression that we were dealing with far more than your usual wannabe gangster warfare."

"Really. How do you mean?"

"I couldn't quite put my finger on it, but it felt bigger than the usual world of gangsters, like someone else was pulling the strings. Someone or something untouchable. A level up if you like."

"A level up from the Talias? I doubt that's even possible? There isn't usually much that can unnerve you, Gia."

"Perhaps not, usually, but I still feel uncomfortable about this mysterious layer that appears to be sitting above the gangster outfit. I fear that your friend William may have got a little too close to understanding what it was all about and for that he paid the ultimate price with his life.

"Now with all due respect we are a much tougher thorn to pull from anybody's side in comparison to your friend, William and perhaps unlike him we didn't attempt to seek any answers to any questions. But in order to protect our stake and control in Birmingham, not to mention our reputation, for us we had to do something very rare."

"What did you do?"

"We joined forces with London, Liverpool, Manchester, Newcastle and Glasgow to form a formidable unit against any attempted penetration into our respective empires. If they needed to take one empire down then they would have to try and take us all down. The stance paid off, but even then, I think we could have been defeated."

"Really, you think so? Fuck me, that would have taken some doing."

"Well, I guess that's why they did seem to recognise the challenge that we had set them. It would have been a war where they wouldn't have escaped with their fair share of casualties and a war like that may have been too much of a distraction for them. So anyway, we came to an agreement with this enemy that was swarming our shores and we based it on the mutual core values of UK gangsters."

Judd wasn't entirely sure if gangsters of any kind had any core values! Nevertheless, he opted not to air his opinion.

Gia continued. "We told them that we didn't much care for their practice of human trafficking, so if they agreed for the human trafficking to stop, then in return, we would all turn a blind eye to the other less worrying criminal activity that was taking place. For a nominal cut of the profits, of course."

"Of course."

"It was bravado but it just about paid off. They probably thought that it was an easy arrangement to implement – the cut of money I'm sure is a drop in the ocean to their operation, which as I have stated I suspect is being run from somewhere else upon high. Nevertheless, I think they perceived us to be a risk that was far easier to tolerate than to terminate."

"Where are they operating in Birmingham?" asked Judd.

"Why do you want to know?"

"Just, because."

"You're not seriously going to go after them, are you? Have you not listened to anything that I've been telling you? Judd, these guys are animals."

"If they're animals then I'll be fine. It's humans we have to be wary of."

"Judd, I'm being deadly fucking serious. They won't think twice about slicing you in half or feeding your balls to their pets. And they will take great pleasure in doing it slowly."

"I appreciate the concern, Gia. I really do. But they may have killed my best friend and they could be holding a young girl against her will who I'm being paid to find. I won't do anything stupid but I'm afraid I have got to do something."

By now Gia was somewhere between feeling angry and incredulous. "No fucking way am I telling you where they are. In fact, I'm not telling you anything else."

Judd smiled and took a step towards displaying the

charm offensive. "Please, Gia. For old time's sake."

"It's for old time's sake that I'm not telling you, you stupid prick."

"My goodness. Gia Talia has a heart. Who would have thought it?"

Gia couldn't help but smile at that remark. "Judd come on, it's not a good idea that you go after them."

"Like I said, I need to do something. I'll be careful. You know me I can look after myself."

Gia paused for a moment. "Ok, I can see you are not going to let this go. But you are going into this with your eyes wide open, right?"

"Right."

"Ok, in truth I suspect that the human trafficking didn't stop, they just got better at hiding it from us and well, if they thought that we didn't know then the understanding between us would never be in jeopardy. Even we don't want to go after them again, Judd. It's not a war that we would relish either. We don't want any boats rocked; do you understand?"

"If I rock any boats it'll be my own one-man dinghy."

"It's your funeral and I won't even come to pay my respects at it either, as you clearly place no value on your own life or my advice."

"Understood."

"Ok, a lot of the girls never get to see daylight so I'm told. And I did hear a rumour that there are some girls being held and therefore 'provided' for punters within the old Tea Chest pub, but obviously I'm not in a position myself to fully corroborate that."

"The Tea Chest? It was boarded up the last time I looked at it."

"Exactly. Perfect for an illegal brothel then wouldn't you say?"

"Thanks, Gia. You've been really helpful."

"Judd, just promise me one thing."

"What?"

"Please, be careful."

CHAPTER 23
HELLO LITTLE GIRL

Judd knocked on the boarded-up door of what had once been the entrance to the Tea Chest pub. He needed to knock a second time and wait in the drizzling rain for a couple more minutes before somebody finally answered.

"What do you want?" came the gruff and unwelcoming voice.

Judd wasn't good at differentiating accents between some countries and placed the accent as being Eastern European. Either Romanian or Polish perhaps. Due to the olive skin on the towering man he plumped for the former.

"I have money to pay for a girl," said Judd.

"There are no girls here."

"Of course, there are. Look I told you I can pay."

"I said, no girls here."

The door had not opened more than six inches during this whole exchange.

"Ok, so I know how this usually works. You have to be careful; I get that. This place isn't exactly advertised in the Yellow Pages, I get that too. I could be a policeman knocking on your door but it's really ok. Didn't Gazmend

116

tell you I was coming? Head like a sieve that dumb fuck. He said he would put my name on the door and you guys would ensure I'd have the time of my life with one of your girls. Never mind there's plenty of other places I can go and get my kicks to stop this money burning a hole in my pocket. I'm sorry I bothered you." Judd turned to leave.

"Wait. Gazmend, the Albanian?"

"Yeah, that's him," said Judd turning back. "He's a good friend of mine." Judd recollected how two nights earlier he had watched Gazmend leave the boarded-up pub and he had then followed him for a few miles back to his family home. It was there that Judd had approached him and the conversation went something like this:

"Barney, long time no see," Judd had said.

"Who the fuck is Barney?"

"Barney, it is you isn't it? I know it's been a while. Maybe twenty years or more but you haven't forgotten me that soon have you?"

"I'm not fucking Barney. Now fuck off."

"Not Barney? My god you look just like him. Who are you then if you're not Barney?"

"My name is Gazmend, not fucking Barney."

"Oh, I'm sorry friend. My mistake, enjoy the rest of your evening." And it had been as easy as that, saving Judd the job of sinking to blackmail tactics by threatening to let Gazmend's wife and daughter in on his sordid little secret.

Back at the Tea Chest, the man at the door stepped aside to allow Judd to step in. For the first time Judd could see more than half the man's face and just how wide his shoulders and biceps were.

On closing the door behind them, the muscled man slammed Judd face-first against the wall and searched him. Once he felt a bulk in Judd's pocket, he pulled out Judd's wallet. Taking a few seconds to inspect the contents he finally spoke.

"Ok you're clean, Mr Starr, friend of Gazmend."

Judd had taken the necessary precautions to carry a

fake driving license and credit cards in the name of Amadeus Starr.

"What type of girl you like?" came the Romanian accent again.

"Most girls appeal to me really, but how about a girl from the Mediterranean. We all have a type don't we, big fella? A Spanish girl perhaps?"

The muscle head appeared slightly perturbed. "What makes you think we have Spanish girls here?"

"Well I don't, especially. I simply answered your question on the hope that you had a Spanish girl, that's all. I can settle for Romanian if that's all you have, but they're ten a penny no doubt. No offence, of course."

Judd was brusquely handed back his wallet. "Follow me."

Next, Judd was led up a makeshift corridor which he could tell had been hastily put together using partition walls from cheap materials. He soon came to a door on his left. The towering muscle head unceremoniously booted the door open.

Sitting on the bed was a dark-haired girl. She barely looked awake. Judd surmised that she had been given heroin or some other type of hard drug. He figured this would have been to easily keep her under control and most likely to ensure that the craving for any drug-habit that she possessed would make her behave herself.

"This is Ravesa. She's the closest looking thing to Spanish that we have. It will be £125 for an hour. For that money she will let you do anything you want to her."

Judd felt disgusted at such treatment of a girl and it took all of his willpower to resist from striking this unfeeling wanker that stood before him square in the face.

"You pay the money up front to me, I come back in an hour."

"Of course," Judd paid the money. "I assume I can have the door closed?"

The muscle head just smirked at Judd and then closed

the door, leaving Judd and Ravesa alone in the room.

Judd made his way over to the girl and sat next to her. He looked around the room and noticed that it didn't have any windows. A lamp was situated in the corner and an electric radiator was plugged in nearby. Washing facilities were absent and he assumed that they must be communally available in another part of the building. He certainly hoped they were anyway for Ravesa's sake.

"Hello there, Ravesa isn't it?"

The girl's head hung low but she was able to nod in affirmation. Then she managed to look up at Judd, her eyes were narrowed and slightly glazed. She was a pretty girl. "I'm sorry, sir. I'm very tired. You want sex?"

"Erm, no, I don't, actually" answered Judd.

"No?" she answered with an air of puzzlement in her weak voice.

Judd pulled out a photograph from inside his overcoat.

"Do you know this girl, Ravesa?"

Ravesa looked at the photo before nodding. "It's Rosa."

"You know her? That's awesome. Good girl. Is she still here, Ravesa?"

"No, she left."

Judd felt a pang of disappointment. "Where too?"

Ravesa shrugged? "I think she went with Larz."

"Who's Larz?"

"He's one of them."

"He's a pimp?"

Ravesa nodded again.

"Ok Ravesa, you've been very helpful. Look I refuse to leave you here like this. I'm going to stand up and I want you to put your arm around my waist. Do you think you can manage that?"

Ravesa nodded.

"Good. I'm taking you out of here."

Ravesa suddenly seemed to snap into a bit more life. "Are you a crazy man? They'll kill me if I try to leave here."

"Is that what Larz did to Rosa? Did he…Did they kill her?"

"No, I heard them talking. I couldn't hear everything but they mentioned how Larz had betrayed them. People used to pay a lot of money for Rosa. She was known as the special one. Spanish girls are not usually found in these sorts of places."

It did puzzle Judd how Rosa had become mixed up with this seedy underworld. Spain was not the usual type of country to fall victim to human trafficking. Perhaps Vina's cousin had a drug habit? But Vina had never said anything like that, but then again, she may not necessarily know.

"No Mr Starr, Spanish girls are not usually found in these places, are they?"

Judd looked towards the doorway and the muscle head and another man, somewhat smaller and wearing a suit, were both standing there. It was that second man who spoke again.

"Your interest in the Spanish girl made Vlad here a little suspicious. And the fact that you are not fucking this girl in front of you right now makes me think he was right to be."

"Vlad? Is that really your name? Fuck me are you guys for real?"

The two men didn't answer, instead they just strengthened their stare.

Judd continued. "I just like to chat a bit with the girls first, that's all. I like to get to know them a little better." Judd's words catapulted him back to the time he had been on the trail of Gareth Banks, a serial killer who had killed prostitutes but had chosen not to sleep with them. He had stated in court that he had just needed to engage in conversation with them because he had felt lonely. It had been enough to see him walk free. The irony of the position that Judd now found himself to be in made him shiver.

"Bullshit. Why do you want to know about Rosa?" pressed the smaller man.

Judd stood up; they clearly didn't believe that he was a regular punter.

"Look. Ok, I don't want any trouble, I just want to know where Rosa is."

"Oh really, and we just hand her over to you, just like that?"

"For a large sum of money, yes I think you would."

"You could never offer enough to cover what she could make for us. She was the special one."

"So, I understand. So anyway, she's left with this Larz chap?"

"Apparently so. It seems you have had a wasted trip, Mr Starr. We don't know where she is any more than you do, however the fact that you now know that we exist makes me slightly uncomfortable and I don't believe that I can allow you to leave."

Judd laughed. "Oh, I'm leaving all right and I'm taking this poor girl with me."

"You think so, do you?"

"I know so. You're a pair of lowlife scum doing this to innocent girls."

"You're very naïve Mr Starr, this thing is far bigger than just me and Vlad. You really don't know what you're getting yourself in to here."

"So, enlighten me."

"I'd love to, but I'm afraid it's strictly on a need to know basis. And you already know too much. Vlad, finish him."

Vlad walked towards Judd and as he lifted his hand to strike him, Judd simply stepped to the side and caught the big man perfectly on the jaw causing him to drop in a state of unconsciousness like a huge felled tree. It was one of Judd's favourite fighting techniques.

The guy in the suit couldn't help but look shocked at

the ease in which Judd had dealt with his henchman. Now as Judd moved towards him, he fled from the door. Judd was left with a decision. Either to chase the suit or rescue the girl. He went for the latter and turned to her lifting her over his shoulder in the way that a fireman would carry someone from a burning building.

The girl was surprisingly light and Judd ran out of the door, along the makeshift corridor and was soon outside. He opened the door to his car and placed Ravesa on the back seat.

Judd was just getting into the driver's seat when a bullet whizzed past his ear. He looked over towards the entrance and he could see that two more muscle heads had appeared, who looked remarkably similar to Vlad. They were firing bullets towards him and his car.

Judd was able to start the engine and begin to manoeuvre away at speed but then one of the muscle heads tried to block his escape by placing himself in the path of the car.

Judd simply accelerated into him, which caused the thug to roll over both the bonnet and across the roof, before unceremoniously coming to a halt by smacking his large torso onto the pavement at the rear of the car.

Judd's exit became clearer.

"Stop firing," said suit to the remaining large man. "Let him go, he will keep. We can't attract any attention to this place."

As Judd raced up Islington Row Middleway, he realised that he was perfectly en route to the Rotunda.

He checked his rear mirror. He was confident that he wasn't being followed and the false name of Amadeus Starr should have been enough for the pimps, or whoever they were, to not know that he was in fact Judd Stone PI.

He spoke an instruction to his dashboard. "Phone Yasmin."

On the fifth ring, Yasmin answered.

"Hello."

"Yasmin, I don't have time to explain but meet me at the Rotunda."

"Since when do I work out of hours?"

"It's not exactly work I need you for, Yasmin, but it is an emergency. I need your help. Please don't have one of your awkward militant moments, there isn't time."

"Is Sab, ok?"

"Sab's fine, she should be home later. She will help you with this, err, emergency. So please just move it on over to my place."

"Ok, ok. Keep your hair on. I'm on my way."

"Thank you, Yasmin."

Judd hung up.

He decided that Ravesa could stay with him for a short while until he figured out what to do with her on a more permanent basis.

Not forgetting what Gia had told him, and the words of the suited man, if the operation that he had just witnessed at the Tea Chest pub was just the tip of the iceberg of a much bigger thing, he wanted to find out more before involving the police. Most importantly he needed to be sure that he wasn't inadvertently blocking any tracks that could lead to understanding what had happened to William. And that was more for his own means than anyone else's.

He knew that the girl would be far too frightened to blow the lid on the trafficking and the prostitution even if the police were to become involved, but at least she would now hopefully be kept safe and hidden at his place. Yasmin would help, in spite of her contrariness he knew he could rely on her when it really mattered.

Judd took another look in the rear-view mirror as he manoeuvred the car along Bath Row. All still seemed ok.

Then a voice came from the back seat. "Amsterdam."

"What did you say?"

"Amsterdam. Rosa told me that Larz was planning to take her to Amsterdam."

"Have you told anyone else this news, Ravesa?"

"No. Just you."

Judd smiled. "Good girl."

CHAPTER 24
CARELESS WHISPER

"What do you mean she's not here? Was she even ready to go home?" asked Judd.

"To be honest with you Mr Stone, we wanted to keep your wife with us a little longer. However, the consultant was reluctantly willing to discharge her as long as he could be completely assured that Mrs Stone would receive an acceptable level of care and supervision away from the hospital."

Judd scratched his head. "I don't understand. Has she already gone back to our home in the Rotunda, then?"

The nurse appeared a little anxious. "I'm afraid not, Mr Stone."

"Now I really don't understand," said Judd. "If she hasn't gone home then where has she gone?"

"I'm sorry Mr Stone, she instructed us not to tell you."

Judd was beyond confused and becoming increasingly irritated. "What the actual fuck are you talking about! You will fucking tell me, I'm her fucking husband for Christ's sake."

"I'm sorry, Mr Stone, I really am but we have to

respect the confidentiality of the patient."

Within a small area, Judd began to pace around and tried to gather his thoughts. "This makes no sense. She obviously isn't thinking straight after her injuries and being in a coma for all that time. You should not have discharged her. I want to speak to the consultant."

"Mr Stone, your wife was assessed as being fully mentally competent to make her own decisions. She clearly seemed to be upset about something though and I think that fuelled her determination to be discharged. As for the consultant who authorized her leaving, I'm sorry, he has finished his shift for today and he has also left the hospital."

"Then tell me what fucking golf course he's on and I'll catch up with him there."

"I really am sorry, Mr Stone but I need you to calm down. I don't want to have to call security."

Judd paused for a moment and composed himself. "Wait. You said she would only be discharged if she had guaranteed care and supervision."

"That's correct."

"So, who collected her from the hospital?"

"I'm not at liberty to say."

"Male? Female?"

The nurse sighed. "Female, and that is already more than I should have told you, Mr Stone."

"Female," Judd began to nod with realisation. "Let me guess. The woman who took her. Her skin colouring was similar to Brooke's and she was tall and skinny, right? A mass of hair stuck on her big head? Her pierced nose stuck in the air? I bet she spoke to you like shit as well, didn't she?"

The nurse offered a smile of sorts and a slight nod.

"Of course, it had to be her. Harper. Harper the fucking Harpy. Brooke's adorable big sister."

"She doesn't want to see you, Judd. Now move away from

my property before I call the police."

"Don't be so fucking stupid, Harper. I'm her husband, now let me speak with her."

Harper folded her arms in defiance. "You're no husband to her."

"Now watch your mouth, Harper. Look I don't know what I'm supposed to have done but perhaps if I talk to her, I can sort this out."

"No way."

"Come on, be reasonable. I need to take her home and look after her, she's been through a lot."

"She doesn't need anything from you, Judd. Nor does she want anything from you neither, although if I were her, I'd bleed you dry for every one of your miserable pennies."

"This is really getting out of hand. I need to speak with my wife."

Suddenly Brooke appeared at the door. She had a crutch under each arm.

Harper got in first. "You need to go back to bed, little sister. You need your rest."

"It's ok, Harper," answered Brooke. "It's clear that he isn't going to go away until I speak with him. Just give me a couple of minutes, he'll soon be gone when I put him straight on a few things."

"Ok," said Harper reluctantly. "I'll just be in the hallway. If he gets all Neanderthal on you just holler."

"It's fine, really. Thanks Harper."

Harper threw Judd a look that could cut ice and grudgingly left the couple to front each other out. Judd couldn't resist a sarcastically fuelled parting shot. "Thanks, Harper, always a pleasure."

Brooke appeared less than impressed.

"What is this all about babe," said Judd. "What's happening here?"

"Don't you dare babe, me."

Wow, Brooke really was pissed at him.

"I don't get it, Brooke. Talk to me."

"Did you miss me while I was in hospital, Judd?"

"What kind of a question is that? Of course, I missed you. I sat with you for hours upon hours, stroking your hand and face, kissing your sleeping eyes, hoping you'd come back to me."

"Really?"

"Really."

"But not all the time?"

Judd hesitated. "Well most of the time. You know I had to work, see to Mr. Mustard and stuff. Oh, I also finally got myself to attend a Gambler's Therapy class. I wanted to make you proud of me once you returned"

Brooke forced a sardonic laugh. "Proud of you?"

"Yes, where is all of this coming from, Brooke?"

"It's a shame you didn't sign up to sex-addicts therapy too."

"Huh?"

Brooke positioned one of the crutches under her armpit so that she could free her hand to search in the pocket of her dressing gown. She pulled out her mobile phone, messed with a selection of digits and turned the screen to face Judd once she had found what she needed.

At first, he couldn't understand why Brooke would be showing him what seemed like a clip from a porn movie, but then his jaw dropped as he recognised the curtains and the décor of the room displayed on the screen. There was no mistake, it was Vina's bedroom and the two people wrapped around each other in the footage also looked familiar. Too familiar.

"Are you going to deny that's you, Judd? And don't try and bullshit me that its ancient footage because I can see the gunshot wounds on your body."

Judd looked to the floor. "It was a mistake, Brooke. I'm sorry."

"Sorry you've been caught, you mean."

"That's not true. Let's talk this through. We can sort this out, Brooke."

"Drop dead, Judd. You have fucked me over one time too many. This time we're over for good."

Judd realised it was futile to do anything other than walk away from the door that had just been slammed in his face.

CHAPTER 25
AMSTERDAM

"You can't avoid my calls forever, Vina," said Judd for the umpteenth time into Vina's voicemail. "I just want to know why you felt you had to do it. Why send Brooke that little home video of yours? It was cruel and unnecessary… Anyway, I'm still going to find Rosa. For her sake not yours, then I want my money and then I don't want to see you ever again." With extreme frustration Judd ended the call.

As well as constantly connecting with Vina's voicemail, the same thing was happening every time he tried to reach Brooke too. It was painfully obvious that his wife didn't want to speak with him either, no matter how often he expressed the word 'sorry' on her phone's memory. The distinct feeling of rejection didn't deter him from trying time and time again though.

After hanging up the line to Vina, Judd walked up the steps of the hotel that he had booked in Amsterdam, checked in at the desk, dumped his case in his hired room and immediately went on his quest to locate Rosa. He figured the quicker he could find the missing girl then the quicker he could break ties with Vina. Any temptations in what the legendary coffee shops may offer him would simply have to wait.

Judd realised that his most likely starting place for success would have to be Amsterdam's notorious Red-light district. He was convinced that this would be the most logical platform where Larz would be pimping out Rosa.

As he meandered through the ancient streets of the neighbourhood of De Wallen, Judd wouldn't have been human if he hadn't been drawn to the beautiful girls parading in the full-length windows of their single rooms. The red-coloured illumination cast a scarlet haze across the whole environment and served to complement the scantily clad bodies on show, regardless of any sense of seediness.

Judd forced his mind to take a step back. He wondered what the individual stories of these girls could possibly be and how they had each found themselves to have arrived at this existence.

Could it be that some simply liked to do it? A small minority perhaps, but he surmised that few girls would willingly put themselves forward for such a career choice.

In fact, he wondered if any of them had actually ever been given a choice? And even for those who had, the weight of influence from other quarters must have lay heavy.

How many had been trafficked?

How many had been falsely promised a better life from the one they had been previously living in the likes of Thailand or Africa?

How many had been blackmailed or threatened?

How many were being controlled by unscrupulous gangsters or pimps?

He knew that Amsterdam deployed more stringent protective protocols for sex workers than other cities, but even so, such questions hung heavy on Judd's mind.

Some of the girls on offer danced, some smiled, some

didn't and some just stood still.

All sorts of nationalities were on offer.

Every colour of underwear was on show. And every style of hair.

Judd noticed one girl wearing spectacles to portray what he took to be the 'naughty secretary' look. She smiled at Judd as he stared at her before she seductively placed her index finger between her bright red lips. He had to admit to himself that she was drop-dead gorgeous and his stomach couldn't help but do an excitable flip. Resisting temptation, he politely smiled at her and moved on as he continued to scour the windows in the hope of spotting Rosa.

At his next encounter, Judd quickly turned away from a girl that wore a parodied school uniform, the skirt cut much shorter than the norm and the school blouse much lower. Judd was more broad-minded than most but nevertheless that image was far too uncomfortable for him considering what it was attempting to portray.

Judd estimated that De Wallen must have had about three hundred or so single room cabins scattered amongst its narrow walkways and streets. After passing about forty of them, he decided to stop at one.

It dawned on him that these rooms were most likely occupied by girls who worked shift patterns, so even if Rosa was working in Amsterdam's red-light district, it was possible that she may not even be available this evening. He needed to start making some enquiries.

By this time, Judd's captivating stroll had led him along the edge of the river Amstel.

He had spotted a girl of potentially Spanish appearance standing behind the glass of her respective premises. Her origin led him to believe that she may be well placed to know of Rosa's whereabouts. Not used to approaching a lady of the night in such a starkly exposed environment, Judd approached the doorway somewhat nervously. He was greeted by a girl of both beauty and confidence.

"Hello," she said smiling. The way she spoke was just as infectious as her looks.

"Hello, may I come in?"

"That's the idea. Is this your first time in Amsterdam?"

"It's that noticeable, huh?"

"Do you want to know price?"

"Err, perhaps we can discuss that inside?" Judd found himself taking a swift look around him, for some reason expecting to find people staring at him or even pointing and laughing at him. He needn't have worried; there was no-one particularly interested in Judd and his movements. After all, a man speaking with a scantily clad lady in her doorway was hardly an unexpected occurrence in this particular part of Amsterdam. Suddenly, Judd had never felt so British.

"That's not how it works, sweetie. I need to know what you want before entering."

"What I want?"

"Sure," she replied in her seductive accent, frowning slightly in puzzlement. "The money needs to be paid to me up front too. Fifty euros for ten minutes, one-hundred euros for half an hour. You can have an hour for one hundred and seventy-five if you can last that long," she took a moment to look Judd up and down. "Actually, you look like a man that could last that long."

"Thanks, you're very kind, but I'll give you one hundred and twenty for just half an hour of your time."

"Ok, it's your money. I'll help you decide what you want, but no putting it in my back door and you use a condom."

"Back doo…oh I get it, no of course not," Judd pulled the crisp notes from his wallet and handed them to the girl.

"Ok, you come in please."

The girl would have been quite tall even if she hadn't been wearing such high-heeled shoes. The ease in which she walked in them was impressive and seemed well-rehearsed as she moved elegantly towards the window to close the curtains for privacy.

Judd couldn't help but stare at her beautifully shaped backside. With every sultry step, the plump but firm cheeks came close to hypnotising him and the high cut of her lace knickers made the most of showcasing her rear asset.

When she turned around, Judd found himself marveling at her equally impressive breasts, which were just about managing to be held aloft by more pretty white lace.

"My name is Ecstasy."

"I have to say, that's a very appropriate name for you."

"Thank you."

She became confused as Judd managed to break his stare away from her beauty and fumble about in his wallet again.

"You already pay."

"No, no I'm not getting out any more money. I have a photograph of a girl I think is working in Amsterdam, could you take a look please and tell me if you know her?"

Judd handed the photo to Ecstasy and to her credit she took the time to study it. "I'm sorry, I don't recognise her. I haven't been working here very long. She may work here but I don't know her, I'm afraid. What you want with her?" Her broken English continued to occasionally remove the use of irregular verbs, but the way she spoke only continued to add to her appeal.

"She's missing."

"I'm sure plenty of girls here are being missed by someone."

"True, but I have to find this girl. In fact, it's actually my job to find her. She may be with a bad man."

Ecstasy looked at the photograph again and considered it with an invigorated interest. "I'm very sorry, I really do not know her." She handed the photo back to Judd.

"Never mind, I just assumed that you may do, as you're

Spanish."

The girl smiled. "I'm not Spanish, I'm Brazilian. Like the way I cut my hair." The girl moved her hand between her legs to signal what she meant.

Judd found himself swallowing hard. "Oh, I see. Err, thank you for your time, but that's all I needed to know. If you knew the girl in the photo that is."

"You pay for half hour."

"I know, but it's ok. You can keep the money."

She moved closer to Judd and began to undo his shirt.

"You pay for half hour; you get half hour."

As she began to unbutton his trousers, Judd concluded that it would have been rude to protest any further.

Judd realised that if he were to continue with the same strategy that had resulted in him engaging in a close encounter with Ecstasy, he would soon not only be broke, but worn out too. Boy, that lady had certainly made sure that he had got his money's worth.

And in spite of their current estrangement, Judd now had a fresh angle of guilty feelings for cheating on Brooke. Again.

His decision to therefore participate in a tour of a historic sex club, guided by a retired and seasoned Amsterdam sex worker, had been an unlikely but smart one. Once the tour was over, he charmed his way to spend some extra time with Greta and shared a platonic drink with her. It paid off; she was able to tell Judd what he wanted to hear.

"Yes, I know this girl. I forget her name but I know that she is with Larz."

"You know Larz?"

"Yes, I know Larz. I was a madame of one of Amsterdam's most popular brothels for over thirty years. I ran a legitimate business mind you, but once you've been in that line of work around here, there isn't much that goes on that can slip by you unnoticed. The red-light district almost becomes the hub of all things Amsterdam if you will." Like a lot of Dutch people, Greta spoke the English language exceptionally well. "Tell me, why do you want to know where this girl is again?"

"Her cousin is looking for her," answered Judd.

"Well if she wanted to be in touch with her cousin, then surely, she would do so of her own accord."

"She may not be able to. Her cousin feels that she may be here in Amsterdam against her will."

The older woman nodded knowingly. "Larz is a nasty piece of work. It could be dangerous for me to speak with you about him and this girl."

"Please, if you can help me to find this girl, I'd be very grateful. Larz will never know that I've spoken with you. I promise."

Greta moved the glass that hosted her gin and tonic to her lips, buying time to weigh up if she should offer her help or not. "He has been in and out of the scene in Amsterdam over the years. Here one minute, gone the next. Like a yo-yo or how do you English say, like a bad penny turning up. The last time he left this country he left under a cloud; I'm surprised he came back to be honest but I have definitely seen him and he was with this girl. There's no mistake."

"He left under a cloud; you say?"

"He was said to owe people money. Money to people that are even scarier than him, but alas those people are no longer in Amsterdam either. That's probably why he has felt that he could return, but his sense of shame should have been enough to keep him out of this city for good." She paused for some more gin and tonic.

"Go on, Greta."

"There was a spate of killings amongst the underworld here. Gangsters fighting to be top dog. Non-Dutch people have moved into the city wanting a piece of the action so to speak. They're a mean bunch. Behind the coffee shops, quaint museums and the swarms of disrespectful cyclists,

Amsterdam can be a dangerous place if you go looking for it."

"Actually, the cyclists are pretty dangerous in their own right," said Judd. "You take your life in your own hands stepping off the pavement around here."

"You've noticed, huh?"

"Hard not to."

Greta smiled momentarily, but then her facial expression soon once again reflected the seriousness of her revelations. "Anyway, the man who I know Larz owed money to was killed, he lost his place on the ladder and I guess that's why Larz has come back."

"It makes sense."

"He's been flexing his muscles around town with this particular girl, the one in the photo. He got her working in the strip club but I think he drew the line at pimping her out for sex. He was very cagey about her indeed. Anyway, she no longer works in the strip club, I know that for sure."

"Do you think she's been harmed?" enquired Judd.

"I wouldn't put it past him. Like I said, he can be a nasty piece of work."

"Where can I find Larz?"

Greta looked straight into Judd's eyes. "You have a kind face; I'd love to help you further but do I look like someone who wants to sign her own death warrant? I've perhaps already told you far too much."

"I can pay you."

"Don't insult me."

"Sorry. I'm just desperate to find the girl."

Greta thought about things for a while. "Let me tell you something, I hated Larz's father even more than I do Larz. He too was a nasty piece of work. He was my pimp and he didn't stop there if you know what I mean. If he wanted a piece of me, or any other girl for that matter, he would just take it. And he liked his sex to be rough. The rougher the better in fact. Even now after all these years the thought of what he put me through makes me shudder. He was a controlling and violent bastard. He even had the authorities in his back pocket, so they turned a blind eye to the way he liked to operate. Luckily he eventually got bored of me when the younger girls started to come along."

"I'm sorry to hear all of this, Greta."

"Well I'm pleased to inform you that Larz's father died some years ago. I raised a glass to celebrate that day, I can tell you."

"I don't blame you."

"You know what? I'm too old to be frightened now by the likes of his no-good son. If Larz is inflicting even half the pain on that poor girl that his old man did to me, then he deserves all that's coming to him if you do manage to catch up with him. Just be careful, he isn't just going to hand her over to you like that."

"Don't worry, Greta. I can take care of myself. I'm under no illusion that I may have to get a little violent."

"That's one of the reasons why I'm going to tell you where you might strike lucky. I wouldn't send a lamb to the slaughter, you know. I just hope you're not too late."

"Too late?"

"Like I said, I haven't seen the girl for a long time."

"I'm optimistic by nature."

"Ok then, head on over to the Vondel park area, Oud Zuid. I'm afraid I don't know the exact house but he lives somewhere along Van Eeghenstraat."

"Thank you, you've been very helpful. Take care of yourself, Greta."

"You're very welcome. Good luck, young man."

For Judd to make his way to the Old South area of the city he needed to pass through the museum quarter which included both the Rijksmuseum and the Van Gogh Museum. However, Judd soon discovered that he didn't have to enter either of the famous museums, or even get as far as the museum quarter, if he wanted to lay his eyes on some artwork of the highest quality.

Judd had no particular interest in art and hadn't especially set out to look at any at all that day, but life happens when you're busy making other plans, and as he passed the window of a small independent art shop his eyes couldn't help but fall on a painting that was on display.

The painting was of his favourite musician, John Lennon. Of course, he had seen many images of the ex-Beatle over the years but this portrait was strikingly different.

Judd felt compelled to enter the shop and ask for a closer look. The friendly store owner willingly took it from the window and allowed Judd to hold the gilded frame as his eyes marveled at the portrait.

The artist had chosen not to reimagine one of the most obvious images of Lennon that had been so often adopted by others before, and this served to make the painting even more appealing to Judd. It was clear that at the time of this particular image, Lennon had still been a Beatle. His hairstyle was cut in the famous mop top but was just beginning to show enough signs of creeping into what would eventually become his long hippy-like locks. Judd pitched it to be somewhere around the *Revolver* to *Sergeant Pepper* era but he couldn't be sure.

The artist had cleverly introduced the style of Van Gogh into Lennon's trademark circular lens spectacles. Lennon's eyes had been camouflaged by swirling blue and yellow patterns, similar to that of Van Gogh's intriguing *Starry Night* painting.

Yet the magic of the painting didn't end there.

The background was psychedelic in nature but not too overwhelming to ensure that Lennon's face remained prominent to the piece. There was a nod on the canvas to *Lucy in The Sky with Diamonds* and other discreet images such as the famous red gates of Strawberry Fields, the orphanage in Liverpool that had inspired one of Lennon's most famous Beatles songs.

There were also clouds breaking through with the words 'Imagine', 'Love' and 'Peace' within them, whilst somehow a subtle Van Gogh flavour in the painting was still expertly maintained by the artist.

Judd's eyes followed the immaculate shading on Lennon's face and then he became amazed at the attention to detail that had been attributed to Lennon's very distinct nose. The artist had managed to capture the half-moon like indent that perched above each of Lennon's nostrils. That integral feature, along with the overall curvature of the central bone, helped to shape the elegance of Lennon's nose into that of a regal, human-like beak.

Judd was totally mesmerised by the painting. It was the kind of painting that one could never get bored of looking at and it felt to Judd as though something new would be discovered each time his eyes would ever scan it.

The captivating portrait had been finished off with the artist's signature in white paint. Jovanna van Hendrix.

A removable label placed at the centre of the bottom part of the frame gave the title of the piece: *If Above us is only sky, John must still walk amongst us.*

Eventually, Judd spoke. "I'm certainly no expert but this painting is truly amazing. I've never seen anything like it before. I've got to have it."

"The artist is truly gifted, sir," said the store owner.

"I'll say. Jovanna van Hendrix. Not an artist I'm familiar with, but then again, as I said, I'm hardly an expert on such matters."

"You're unlikely to have heard of her. She is a student at the Amsterdam School of Art. I allow the students to sell pieces of their work in my shop for a small percentage. I respect all of them, but Jovanna is one of the better artists who I help out. If you walk over to the wall on the far left of the shop, I have a few more pieces that have been painted by the students, including more of Jovanna's.

I'll begin to carefully wrap this one up for you while you take a look."

"Are you able to ship the painting to England for me?"

"That won't be a problem, sir."

"That's excellent. Thank you very much."

Judd walked over to the said wall and he could see a number of paintings hanging in a fairly random manner. Quickly scanning the paintings, he checked the signatures and it was definitely those crafted by Jovanna van Hendrix that he was most drawn to.

There were no more portraits of rock stars but that didn't deter Judd from admiring her artwork.

"These should really be in a gallery," said Judd.

"I prefer them in my shop."

"Fair enough," smiled Judd. "I couldn't have purchased that Lennon portrait if it hadn't have been for your shop, now could I?"

Judd decided to take one last scan of the wall of art and suddenly his eyes became fixed on a painting of a silhouetted man with his back facing any would-be admirer of the picture. In this case the admirer was Judd.

The man in the painting was wearing a long coat with the collars turned up and what seemed like a trilby or fedora hat upon his head. He was standing on a hillside of grass akin to Van Gogh's depictions in such paintings as *Mountainous Landscape Behind Saint-Remy* and the figure was looking into a graveyard scattered with strikingly-shaped gothic gravestones. A couple of smaller figures had seemingly dug open a grave and were pulling jewellery from the hand of a hidden corpse. The sky had the same swirly patterns in the style of Van Gogh but the usual blueness had been replaced with shades of grey and black.

The painting was eerie yet deadly captivating. Just as he had been with the unique Lennon portrait, Judd became completely drawn into the painted canvas.

Judd read the title of the piece. *De privedetective.* "Does that translate to The Private Detective?" he asked the proprietor.

"It does indeed, sir."

Judd couldn't believe the coincidence. It felt as if this painting had been painted just for him. "I'll take this one too, please."

"Thank you, I'm very pleased that you entered my shop today. It is a very unusual piece that one. You will notice no doubt some similarity to the work of Vincent van Gogh, but nevertheless the artist maintains her own unique style of using acrylics whereas of course Van Gogh himself favoured oils. The use of acrylic gives more texture and sculpted dimension, don't you think?"

"I just think they're amazing. Truly amazing. I see they are priced at two-hundred euros each. What a bargain."

"You're making a wise investment, sir. Once Jovanna is better known these paintings will be worth considerably more. She'll be very pleased when I tell her that they have sold. Where am I shipping them to sir?" The store owner handed Judd a small piece of paper and a pen. Judd duly wrote down his name and address: The Rotunda, Birmingham, England, included the postcode and handed the pen and paper back to the woman.

"I'm afraid that I'll have to charge twenty-five euros for postage to England, is that ok?"

"That's absolutely fine. Is paying by card ok?"

"Yes, it is. No problem at all."

Judd completed the transaction.

Delighted with his purchase and temporal respite, he bid farewell to the friendly store owner and headed out of the door to continue with his much less-appealing quest.

There were no coffee shops providing the Amsterdam famed 'wacky backy' on the desirable residential street of Van Eeghenstraat, however there was a regular café that sold beverages and pastries. Judd purchased an americano and parked himself in the window seat hoping that Larz or Rosa would walk past at some point. Just over an hour later he got amazingly lucky when they both actually entered the café together.

They each ordered a coffee and nestled at a table towards the centre of the room. In fact, they had sat perfectly in Judd's eye line and he was able to easily yet discreetly surveil them.

At first, they looked like they could have been any other regular couple simply popping in for a coffee, but soon the body language appeared to get a little strained. The look on Larz's face turned to one of thunder whilst Rosa seemed to cower and sink into the collars of her jacket. She even began to close her eyes as if she was trying to hide away from the world.

Judd was no expert on the average pimp and call girl relationship but what was unfolding before him suggested that this was how men like Larz could rule by fear. At one point, Larz grabbed Rosa's wrist. She managed to break free but she made no attempt to raise the alarm or make a run for it.

After about twenty minutes they left the café and headed off down the street. Judd gave it another twenty seconds or so before he too left in order to follow them, keeping just enough distance to ensure that they could not tell that he was tailing them.

It wasn't too long before Larz and Rosa stopped outside one of the houses. It had a large tree outside which helped Judd to make a mental marker for his planned return. They seemed to be arguing. Judd couldn't hear what was being said but once Rosa had unexpectedly slapped his face the large man defaulted to his seemingly preferred tactic of grabbing her wrists. Soon after he dragged her out of sight.

Judd was tempted to pick up pace and intervene there and then but he felt that the timing wasn't quite right. Especially when a woman, seemingly oblivious to the altercation, crossed from over the road taking her French bulldog and Dachshund for a walk, followed by a car driving past and a sweaty jogger appearing from nowhere to overtake Judd. He would return tonight, when it was dark, armed with the element of surprise and without the risk of onlookers or twitching curtains. Then he would rescue Rosa.

The moon was crescent-shaped when Judd walked down Van Eeghenstraat for the second time. He reached the large tree which signaled that he had reached the correct building for his rescue attempt and then he turned a sharp left in order to enter the foyer via the communal entrance. Fortunately, the front door seemed to be permanently propped open by an old wooden door stop, the sort that resembled a slice of cheese. This was an obvious arrangement to make entering the building convenient for the residents but it significantly compromised the security of the place.

Judd made his way across the marble floor, crept up the first flight of stairs and promptly kicked the door into his targeted apartment.

Realising that the apartment had been renovated within a typical historic Amsterdam house he knew that the residence would only have the two rooms, so by attacking at night he instantly turned left to make his way into the bedroom.

Judd fired his torch into life but when shining it upon the double bed he was surprised to discover that it lay empty. There was no Rosa and no six-foot five-inch Neanderthal male with a crew cut.

Naturally, Judd needed to re-evaluate his course of action and as he turned to leave the room, he found a coffee cup being smashed against his skull, causing hot but fortunately not boiling liquid to spill all over him.

Although dazed, Judd's adrenaline refused his entire state of consciousness to concede defeat and he quickly countered by striking the torch across the hard skull that hosted the familiar crew cut.

The fight spilled into the area that served as both a living room and a kitchen with both men trading punches and wrestling holds, neither wanting to allow a millisecond of vulnerability which the other could potentially exploit.

Judd managed to connect with a telling punch which jerked his large opponent's head backwards and it hit the ceiling lampshade causing it to swing back and forth. The light had been left on from when the cup of coffee had not long been made and the movement of its swing produced an alternating, shifting pattern of darkness and light across the room. This provided an interesting backdrop for the fight which was lost on any would-be spectators.

Eventually, Judd was able to overpower his opponent, although he had to accept that this man-of-steel was one of the most capable fighters that he had ever come up against.

With the large man lying on the floor, writhing in agony and exhaustion, Judd himself pretty breathless and sore, was quick to grab a large knife from the kitchen area to ensure that his opponent stayed where he was.

"Ok, where is she?"

"Where's who?" replied a Dutch accent.

Judd drew a kick into the side of the floored man causing him to yell in pain.

"You know who, Rosa."

"She's not here."

"Evidently, so what have you done with her?"

"She's far away from you and anyone else who wants to harm her."

"What the fuck are you talking about? You're her kidnapper. Now, where is she?"

The large man started to laugh as blood trickled from the corner of his mouth.

"What's so funny?"

"Is that what they told you? You dumb fool. I thought that you were one of them but as I don't recognise you it's clear to me now that they must have hired you."

"You had better start making sense, pal. I have been hired by the family of Rosa and they expect me to bring her home. So, where the fuck is she?"

"Rosa's family? That's who has hired you?"

"Err yeah, that's what I said. Who else?"

"That means only one thing. Vina has sent you. She's almost as bad as them."

"As bad as who?"

"The fuckers I rescued Rosa from. You're either jerking me off or you've only been told half the story…Pal."

"Keep talking."

"If you think I'm going to let you take Rosa back to Vina you're very much mistaken. She's safer with me. I'd rather die than hand her over. So, if it's a choice of you driving that knife into me versus Vina having her clutches back into her cousin then go right ahead."

Judd was beginning to discover that things were not as he necessarily understood them to be. "You're Larz, right?"

"I might be."

"As I thought. Ok Larz, I'm going to sit over here and I'm going to allow you to stand up and sit over there by the window. Now don't try anything funny or I won't hesitate to put this knife straight into you time and time again. Do you understand?"

Larz didn't reply, he just gingerly slouched into the chair which gave him some obvious discomfort. He held his side in a vain attempt to ease the pain and his left eye was completely closed with severe swelling. His nose was clearly broken too.

"What's the story then Larz? If I'm led to believe that you have Rosa's best interests at heart why did she slap you across the face earlier today."

"You saw that?"

"Yes."

"She's a feisty girlfriend. We had a quarrel, that's all."

"You expect me to believe that you're actually in a relationship with Rosa?"

"You can believe what you want to believe. All I know is I'm not handing her over to you or anyone else."

"How do I know that she's not dead? What was her punishment for slapping you earlier? I saw you grab her and drag her into the building. I knew that I should have kicked your arse right there and then."

"Sometimes Rosa needs controlling. I used a bit of force on her, it's true but did you see me strike her like she struck me?"

"No, I can't say that I did, but that could have been because you were in public and once you had her behind closed doors then it became a different matter."

"You're wrong. I just wanted to ensure that we made up, before she went on her trip. She refused to let me go with her which worries me deeply. I just want to protect her, she's been through a lot, but Rosa still likes her own space."

"A little too much for your liking."

"Perhaps. She thinks I'm possessive but like I said I just want to protect her."

"And that's why you argued, she wanted to travel alone. Without you?"

Larz nodded. "I worry what could happen to her. I thought she would be safe here in Amsterdam, with me and with her new name, but now it turns out that you were able to find us. Now we'll have to start again. It's a good thing she has gone away for a short while it would seem. You've missed her."

Judd was finding it difficult to doubt Larz's sincerity.

"So, if Rosa isn't in danger from you, then who is she in danger from?"

"Apart from you, you mean?"

"Larz, let me assure you that Rosa is in no danger from me. You have my word. I only want to help Rosa. Tell me your story, come on. I'm a good listener. Look, I'm putting the knife down."

Larz sighed. "Okay. What does it matter now anyway? I was part of the gang that processed girls into the UK."

"Processed? You mean trafficking, don't you?"

"I don't like to use that word."

"But still…"

Larz nodded.

"Where are these girls from?"

"Eastern Europe mainly, it was unusual for us to get Rosa."

"Someone from Spanish origin?"

"Yes. Rosa made me see things differently. I was disgusting. She made me see who I really was, just by her existence. She's a very special person. I became very ashamed. Until she came, I didn't see those girls as human beings with feelings and families. I saw them as products that I could make a lot of money from. It shouldn't have taken Rosa to make me wake up and smell the coffee as they say, but she was special and she made me realise that it was all wrong."

"So, what happened?"

"I rescued her and brought her to Amsterdam."

"To work in the red-light district?"

"Of course not."

"Why else would you bring a young girl to Amsterdam. You've just picked up where you left off. You're her fucking pimp, aren't you?"

"You insult me."

"Well boo-hoo."

Larz noticed Judd hover his hand over the resting knife. That fact, coupled with his lack of energy, made him reconsider going for Judd again.

"I'm her boyfriend. We came to Amsterdam to set up a new life and so Rosa could follow her dream. I know Amsterdam, it was my home long before I got involved with those crooks. Here I thought I could protect her."

"Follow her dream? Earlier you said that she was using a different name."

"Like I'm going to tell you."

"You may not have sent her out into the Red-Light district but I know you had her stripping."

"You know a lot."

"It's my job."

"Stripping wasn't something either of us wanted for Rosa, but we had to make money fast. Once I re-established my reputation again in Amsterdam using my family name, I pulled her away from stripping as quickly as I could and I set up a nice home here for us in Oud Zuid. Pimps do not live in Oud Zuid."

"But gangsters do it would seem."

"I hated her stripping. I admit I run a few protection rackets, it's true but that's all. Let me tell you the people I target aren't exactly saints. And while I do that yes, Rosa follows her dream."

Judd inadvertently glanced over Larz's shoulder and something caught his eye. Next to the window a painting was hanging. And just like the paintings that he had purchased from the art shop, he spotted that the painting had a Van Gogh feel about it. It was a portrait. Not of a musician, but this was an intimate painting of Larz. The artist had captured Larz's chiseled features and square jaw perfectly.

Then as he lowered his eyes along the painting and slightly squinted, he could make out the artist's signature. It had been signed by Jovanna van Hendrix.

A million pennies suddenly dropped.

"Fuck me, Rosa is Jovanna van Hendrix. I actually purchased a couple of her paintings earlier."

"You did?"

"She's a talented artist."

"She's a talented artist, a talented musician and a truly wonderful human being. I told you, she's a very special person."

"A musician too, you say. Like Vina?"

"Yeah like Vina. The fucking bitch."

"So, tell me. Why do you hate Vina so much?"

"Was it Vina that hired you?"

"Yes, to bring her cousin back safe and sound. I aim to do just that."

"If you take her back to Vina then you will be sending her straight back into trouble."

"How do you mean?"

One more penny was about to drop.

"It was Vina who sold her own cousin to the gangsters. She wants you to find her so that she can do it all over again. She's pissed that Rosa got away and no doubt that doesn't look good on Vina. Like I said everyone saw Rosa as a special girl – for different reasons. Who knows perhaps those gangsters are giving Vina a non-negotiable instruction to get her cousin back to them if you know what I mean? And that means she may be paying you but she's also using you."

"So where is Rosa now?"

"Do you really think that I'm going to tell you that? I don't even know who you are, other than you've been hired by a woman who I wouldn't trust as far as I can throw her."

"But you can trust me. My name is Judd Stone. Look, you would rather have been with her, to protect her, I get that now. You've helped me see everything in its true light, Larz. I swear that I won't take her back to Vina if it's not the right thing to do. Believe me Vina's not my favourite person at the moment either. Let me go to where Rosa is. I'll look after her for you, like I said, you can trust me."

"How can I trust a man who has broken my nose?"

"You smashed a hot cup of coffee over my head."

"You broke into my house."

"Fair comment, but all of that was before I knew the truth. Look, if I have been able to track you down to Amsterdam how do you know that Rosa is safe now, where ever she is? There may be others looking for her and they will be looking to do her harm. Not like me. Tell me where she is and I swear I'll bring her back to you safe and sound."

Larz thought about Judd's offer for a moment.

"Ok, I will tell you. I don't like to think of her out there alone, that's for sure. Even now she likes to be a stubborn and independent woman. But if she comes to harm, I will find you and I will kill you Mr Judd Stone."

"That's fair enough Larz. I only want to help you and Rosa."

"Ok, I will tell you. Listen carefully."

"I'm listening, Oh by the way, I'm sorry about your nose. It will heal in time."

CHAPTER 26
PRAGUE

After being entertained in the truest sense of the word by Jovanna van Hendrix, Judd left his seat in the St Francis of Assisi Church in awe of her performance.

The impressively structured church, positioned at one end of the Charles Bridge in Prague, hosted a regular programme of classical concerts, but few could ever rival the brilliance of Jovanna van Hendrix's virtuoso performances.

The captivating musician had been positioned aloft to the east of the church simply because that's where the organ that had been built in 1702 was situated – the very same organ that had once been played by the composer Wolfgang Amadeus Mozart. In fact, Jovanna van Hendrix had probably been the most talented musician to have hit the keys of that organ since Mozart himself.

On this particular evening, Jovanna had actually played an organ solo composed by Mozart called 'Marriage of Figaro Overture'. She sandwiched the piece between Ludwig van Beethoven's 'Moonlight Sonata', bravely yet refreshingly played on the organ as opposed to its intended instrument of the piano, before she stood and faced the audience from on high, changed her instrument of choice from organ to violin and impressively finished her set with a selection of Niccolo Paganini's 'Caprices'. 'Caprices' is often referred to as one of the most difficult and challenging violin pieces that there is to play, fueling many rumours that the extraordinary Italian composer had been in league with the Devil himself.

Jovanna had worn dark glasses for her performance, which when coupled with her ability to display such outstanding techniques with ease such as pizzicato, parallel octaves and arpeggios or scales at great pace, seemed to add to the spectacle that her performance appeared almost otherworldly.

The versatility and competence of Jovanna van Hendrix's approach to her instruments had simply been astounding.

Judd had been hooked from the beginning, recognising 'Moonlight Sonata' as one of the few classical pieces that he could actually name. Most of that, however, had been owed to his knowledge that John Lennon had used the instrumental structure of the sonata backwards in order to compose the Beatles' track 'Because'. From the moment Jovanna played the first few bars of the piece it was impossible for Judd not to be in awe of the nimble fingers that danced about the organ keys and later the violin strings with animated brilliance.

Now the recital was over, Judd stepped outside of the Baroque-dated church and waited for the musician to inadvertently follow him, which was a good twenty minutes or so later.

Judd had kept himself amused by raising his head to admire the church's magnificent dome and then casting an eye towards the boats travelling up and down the river Vltava. He also enjoyed watching the hordes of people, tourists and locals, swarming in and around Charles Bridge, many indulging in the doughnut chimneys filled with ice cream.

Eventually the talented young woman came into view. "Miss Van Hendrix, may I speak with you please?" asked Judd, trying to look as friendly as he possibly could.

"Is it an autograph that you want?" came the reply in a Spanish accent.

"Not exactly, I very much enjoyed your organ and violin playing though."

"Thank you, it's very kind of you to say. Please excuse me I have things to do."

As the musician began to walk away, Judd knew that he couldn't let the opportunity slip by with her. "Can I take you for a drink around here? There's some bars in and around the old square that are very nice?"

The sheer audacity of the request was enough to stop Jovanna van Hendrix in her tracks. "Are you always this forward with people you meet for the first time? Why would I go for a drink with you? We have only just met?"

Judd smiled, hoping he simply looked friendly and not wacko. "Well, not only do I admire your musical ability I admire your artwork too. I've actually travelled all the way from Amsterdam to meet you after buying two of your paintings."

For the first time Judd saw the lady's eyes as she raised her dark glasses to look at him. "You've purchased my artwork? The ones for sale in Amsterdam?"

"Yes."

"Well thank you again, but are you some sort of an obsessed stalker or something? The strength of two of my paintings doesn't exactly warrant someone travelling across several countries just to meet me. And how did you know I was even here?"

"I beg to differ; your art is amazing. Anyway, Larz told me where to find you."

The Spaniard looked surprised. "No way, Larz would never tell anyone my movements."

"Well we came to an, err, agreement, once he knew

that I knew you were actually Rosa Moreno."

She looked slightly confused and frightened all at the same time. "Who are you? What do you really want? Have you come to harm me? I'm not going back to that life again, no way. I'll scream this bohemian city down if I have to."

"Relax, I'm not here to hurt you, Rosa. My name is Judd Stone. I was hired to find you but not to harm you, I promise. After speaking with Larz I also understand that things are not quite as simple as I had been led to believe by the woman who hired me?"

"Woman? It was my cousin who hired you wasn't it?"

"Yes, it was Vina who hired me. But listen, it is a bit weird how things have turned out because I do genuinely love your art work, which I swear I purchased before I even knew that Jovanna van Hendrix and Rosa Moreno were the same person."

"Really?"

"Really. I'm a huge Beatles fan and I was taken by your Lennon portrait as soon as I laid eyes on it. Believe me, if we go for a drink together then you will not be in safer hands. I was once a bodyguard for a famous musician, so you can trust me."

"Really? Who?"

"Phoenix Easter."

"No way."

"It's true."

"Wow, just wow. She was good. Really good… But then again look what happened to her, she died at the age of twenty-seven and you're telling me that was on your watch? That doesn't exactly fill me with confidence Mr Stone."

"It was, err, complicated, what happened to Phoenix. You have nothing to worry about being with me, I can assure you. Come on, just one drink. You can choose a very public place amongst this very busy city. I just want to hear your side of the story. I'd actually like to help you if I can."

Rosa thought for a moment as her fear subsided.

"So, you're a John Lennon fan."

"Obsessively so."

"Ok I know where we can go."

"This is absolutely amazing. I didn't even know that this existed in Prague and I consider myself to be a more avid fan than most. Thanks so much for bringing me here, Rosa."

"You're welcome."

Rosa had led Judd down the nearby steps of the Charles Bridge and taken him on a short walk along the river. With a couple of twist and turns amongst the Gothic architecture they had come to a wall coated in artwork and graffiti in homage to just one man. John Lennon.

"The artwork isn't quite to the same high standard as yourself of course, Rosa," continued a beaming Judd. "But nevertheless, I fully appreciate the sentiment."

"It's a pretty special place. The John Lennon wall came into existence not long after his death in 1980. It started with just a single painting and poem from an unknown individual."

"Really? And now look at it. Pictures and scribing everywhere."

"That original portrait has long gone. The images get perpetually replaced over time as more and more people want to add something to the wall, and even when the authorities come along and whitewash the lot, pictures and other stuff quickly begin to dominate it once again."

"A similar thing happens to the wall outside Abbey Road studios."

"Such is the legacy of The Beatles, even all these years later huh? John is my favourite Beatle too. It's worth knowing that this wall is not only a pictorial tribute to Lennon, it also celebrates his spirit and a lot of what he stood for."

"How do you mean?" asked Judd.

"Many students have used the wall as a backdrop to fight against communism or other political impositions. For many it has been a platform to liberation and a place where their voice can be heard."

"Yes, that's very Lennon inspired, I can see that,"

"Certainly, more Lennon than Lenin."

"So, if I were to come again in say five years' time, that message over there stating 'All You Need Is Laska' may not even be here or that heavily shaded portrait of the great man next to it?"

"That's correct."

"Well, I'm certainly no artist or poet, but I simply cannot leave here without putting my own small tribute somewhere on that wall, even if it may only be on view for a limited amount of time."

"You know what, Judd? I think you should," Judd watched on as Rosa fiddled about in her handbag. "Here, I always carry a marker with me, I'm afraid it's only black though."

"Black is perfect."

Judd took the marker from Rosa and moved closer to the wall. He had spotted a single white space amongst the psychedelic colours that otherwise swarmed the surface and proceeded to write a very simple message accompanied by a simple cartoon drawing of Lennon, much like the speedy self-portrait depiction that the Beatle often used to doodle himself. Judd's message read "From a Brummie in Prague with love and peace. Keep imagining."

Judd turned to Rosa and smiled. "That'll do it."

"I think it will. Anyway, do you still want to buy me that drink?"

"Of course. It's the least I can do for bringing me here."

"Then I have the very place."

"I still can't fucking believe it. First a John Lennon wall

and now a John Lennon Pub! Here in Prague so many miles away from Liverpool."

"It kind of highlights the universal effect he had."

"Yeah, he certainly touched a lot of people. But you know what Rosa? With your artistic and musical talent so could you."

By this time, Judd had handed over the Czech Koruna in exchange for a dark beer for himself and a double becherovka and tonic for Rosa. The newly acquainted couple sat nestled amidst the various items of Lennon and Beatles memorabilia that dominated the walls, doors and ceiling of the pub. In a salute to The Beatles' Britishness, the pub even had a traditional red telephone phone box installed inside!

"Mmmm, decent beer," said Judd taking a hefty sip and then wiping his mouth with the back of his hand. "So, I get why you needed to use a different name but why Jovanna van Hendrix?"

"Jovanna is Spanish for wanting freedom and for wanting to enjoy life. God knows I needed to try and feel both of those things again. So, the name Jovanna made good sense to me to use, but Larz told me that I should adopt a Dutch surname to dampen any scent for those who would try and track me down. I didn't realise that Hendrix was a Dutch name until I researched the country's surnames. Once I knew its origin, as a fellow musician it made sense to me to use that too. Throwing 'van' into the mix made it seem even more authentic."

"That all seems logical now. In some ways it must be nice to be able choose your own name."

"Depends on the circumstances. It's not much fun if it's to try and stop you being kidnapped. Or worse."

"I guess not. And you study at the Amsterdam School of Art and Design?"

"It's perfect for me. When I'm there and when I'm painting, I get that sense of 'Jovanna'. That sense of freedom. For that time, it is like I am someone else yet it's also like I'm the real me. The me that hasn't been used and abused. I feel the same way when I play my music. I can get lost in the art and music and forget about the horrible things I've been made to do since Vina handed me over to those bastards."

"So Larz was right when he said Vina had sold you to them?"

"Yes, they were willing to pay a lot for a Spanish girl and it got me out of her way. It was a win-win situation for my evil cousin. She has never liked me, even when we were kids."

"Why? Why did she dislike you so much and why would she do that to you? It seems very extreme."

"Vina is a very extreme woman. She is close to being a psychopath let me tell you. How well do you know her, Judd?"

Judd didn't want to fully admit just how close he had got to Vina but he was certainly becoming increasingly aware of her evil streak. "I've seen things of her that are starting to add up. I guess she wanted me to find you simply because she didn't want you to be free, not that she ever told me her true motives."

"And also, while I'm missing, those gangsters will be holding her to account. I'm sure they are making Vina's life very uncomfortable at the moment. And as for her hating me, she was always jealous of my musical ability. I used to tell her that there was room for both of us to shine in this world but that's not Vina's way. She always had to be the centre of attention. You know as kids I actually used to look up to her. I loved my elder cousin, but now, believe me if I never see her again it will be too soon. So, anyway. What are you going to do now that you've found me, Judd?"

Judd took in a sharp intake of breath. "I honestly don't know, but I'm not handing you back to anyone who hasn't got your best interests at heart that's for sure. I said you could trust me and I meant it. I'll probably just leave you to live happily ever after with Larz."

"Do you have to?"

Judd frowned. "I don't understand?"

"Larz is ok, he helped me escape and for that I'll always be thankful. But now looking back I wonder how much of it could be have been attributed to Stockholm Syndrome? Sitting here now talking to you, I know I don't love him and it's as simple as that. He can be a very controlling boyfriend and he has very old-fashioned views on how a woman should behave. Why else do you think I like to get away to Prague every now and again to play concerts."

"Wow, so you don't even want to be with Larz either. So, what are *you* going to do about you, Rosa?"

"I really don't know. I wish that I could just play my music and paint my art but I need to do it from a place of anonymity."

"You've changed your name."

"It's not enough, Judd. I thought it would be but it isn't. I love what I do and I love the joy it brings to others but am I striving for any fame? No, I'm not and especially if it raises my profile to be kidnapped and used for sex all over again."

Judd drank some more of his beer. "Well maybe anonymity and even autonomy is achievable. I mean, who the fuck knows who Banksy is?"

"That's very true," said Rosa, placing down the remains of her double becherovka and tonic on the coaster. "And I remember that he even had an exhibition in Amsterdam."

"Well there you go then."

"But you found me, didn't you Judd? And that's with me being Jovanna not Rosa. So, if you found me then the gangsters could too."

"Look. Vina doesn't know that I have found you, and I can keep it that way."

"That could be very dangerous for you, Judd. If you don't deliver what is expected of you, I don't think you'll be let off lightly. You don't know who she is still mixed up with or who is helping to pull her strings."

"Let me worry about that. Now tell me again, you really would like a life that is safely tucked away from any potential harm while you painted away at your canvas and tinkled away at the old ivories."

"And played my violin, but yes, that would be ideal. Heaven even, but that's easier said than done."

"I may be able to help."

Rosa looked hopeful. "Really, how?"

"I have contacts. I know people who can make people disappear."

"I'm not sure I like the sound of that."

Judd smiled. "Yes, I do know people who can make people disappear in that way, but that's not what I meant. They could also make you disappear with the advantages totally being attributed in your favour."

Rosa frowned. "Well that sounds perfect, but you're having me on, right?"

"I've never been more serious, Rosa. You deserve my help."

"I don't know what you have planned. It sounds crazy and I can't believe I'm saying this after only meeting you today but, what is it you English say? I'm all ears."

"Trust me, I can fix it."

"But how could I ever repay you such an ask?"

"Well you have already taken me to Prague's John Lennon wall and pub, which has certainly helped make up for me missing the Hilton in Amsterdam. I wanted to see where John and Yoko had done their 'stay in bed for peace' campaign but I never had the time. However, there is one more thing that you could do for me which will help me solve a historical jigsaw that I'm building in my mind. I need to know if you're a piece of it, Rosa."

"I'm intrigued. Totally confused but intrigued."

"I wonder if Prague have any good past life regressionists."

"You're a bit weird aren't you, Judd?"

"Trust me, Rosa."

"You know what? Strangely, I do."

"Now let me begin to secure that life of anonymity and autonomy for you."

Judd pulled out his mobile phone, scrolled through the contacts list on his screen and stopped at the contacts stored under the letter 'G'. He dialed the associated number. After three rings it was answered.

"Hi, Gia. It's Judd…Yeah, I'm good thanks… I know someone who could do with your specialist kind of help…I'm willing to help with the finances but I thought you could cut me some slack, for old time's sake. You know, considering our history and stuff…Allow me to explain…"

Judd winked at Rosa and Rosa returned a smile.

"This looks like the place," said Judd stopping at a gothic doorway on Prague's Old Town Square. "I'll knock the door."

"It is certainly in an ideal location," said Rosa. "We are practically opposite the astronomical clock."

"Yes, very nice indeed and perhaps apt too."

"That's kind of where I was coming from."

Judd nodded. "Maybe there is good reason for a regressionist having their office opposite a symbol of old father time. Just think of all the many and varied lives that have passed beneath that old clock face."

The door was answered quickly. Judd and Rosa were greeted by a man of average height and build. His hair was somewhat unkempt and he wore a heavy shadow of stubble on his face, both of which were speckled with grey and white colouring. "Hello, I'm Jan Barkus. Can I help you?"

"Hello, I'm Mr Stone and this is Miss Van Hendrix. We phoned earlier about a past life regression."

"Ahh, yes, yes of course. Please come in."

"Two regressions actually, one each," said Rosa.

"Right, Judd?"

"Right." Judd had reluctantly agreed with Rosa to also undergo a regression, he couldn't see how he could refuse under the circumstances.

"That won't be a problem," smiled Jan.

Judd and Rosa were led into a room where they stood on a floor of tiles. The history of the building radiated from every corner, facet and feature.

"So, who wants to go first?" asked Jan.

"Miss Van Hendrix," answered Judd without hesitation.

Rosa narrowed her eyes towards Judd as a half-joking act of disdain. "Just remember, that you wanted me to do this so you're paying."

"I wouldn't have it any other way."

Rosa was asked to sit down and she was made to feel very comfortable by Jan. As the process of the regression unfolded, Judd observed that Jan's procedure was very similar to that of Sandy's.

Jan guided Rosa through meadows, mountains, oceans and blue skies until she soon fell into a visibly relaxed state accompanied by a steady pattern of deep breathing.

Rosa was then taken down the flight of stairs where each step represented a year of her life.

It soon made uncomfortable viewing for Judd. Rosa stepped off the stairway at various steps of her formative years and it was clear that she had undoubtedly been bullied by her older cousin, Vina. The abuse had seemingly been relentless and came in varying forms. Both physical beatings and mental torture had clearly been suffered at the hands of her older cousin and Judd's anger at this woman, whom he had foolishly chosen to betray his wife with, was becoming almost tangible.

At one-point, Judd had been forced to explain to Jan that Rosa and Jovanna van Hendrix were in fact the same person, as it was beginning to confuse the regressionist. Judd realised that there would be no point in continuing the regression if its integrity was compromised. Jan thanked him for his honesty and assured Judd that all regressions would remain confidential.

The continuation of Rosa reliving her suffering was becoming more and more distressful to watch and Judd felt compelled to intervene. "Jan, this is clearly very painful for her. Is it possible to take her back to the eighteenth century, please? I'm very interested to understand who Rosa was back then for some research that I'm involved with."

"I will try, but regression doesn't work as easily as turning a tap on and off."

"I understand, it would just be very useful if you could migrate to that period of time."

Jan shouldn't have been so modest because pretty soon he had hit the jackpot as far as Judd was concerned.

"Where are you now, Rosa?" asked Jan.

"Rosa, who is Rosa? My name is Samuel Galton."

Samuel Galton!

Judd's ears instantly pricked up. He was sure that he recognised the name as a member of the Lunar Society and quickly searched his mind for confirmation.

Of course, Galton. The gunmaker.

"Hello Samuel, where are you?" continued Jan.

"I'm at home."

"And where is your home, Samuel?"

"Great Barr Hall."

Bingo. Great Barr Hall. The scene of the discovery of the skeleton. So, just as Judd had suspected there has to be a connection with Rosa.

"Are you alone?" asked Jan.

"No, my friends are with me. Matthew and James."

Boulton and Watt. It has to be, thought Judd. He sat forward in his chair, his attention mounting by the second.

"Oh, and he's lurking in the background as always," said Rosa. "The charlatan."

"Who is this charlatan, you speak of?" enquired Jan.

"Silas Hawke."

Judd searched his brain. Not a name he recognised or one he knew to be in connection with the Lunar Society.

"Silas Hawke?" asked Jan aiming to clarify the identity of the perceived charlatan.

"Yes. He's a complete and utter deluded fool. He thinks he is as good as us, if not better. He will always be a footman in my eyes and he should be thankful for that. I pay him more than I do the other servants and maids and he should count himself lucky that I only have him standing around looking handsome most of the time. Perhaps I need to reconsider his duties of employment. The Devil makes work for idle hands to do."

"Why is this man stirring so much hostility in you, Samuel?"

"He wants to be a part of us."

"Us?"

"The Lunar Society, or Lunarticks as we playfully like to call ourselves," Rosa in the guise of Galton smiled for a second but something between annoyance and anger quickly consumed her/him. "He is mad. Mad I tell you. He claims to have the collective skills of all of us. He thinks he is a botanist, a philosopher, an inventor, a scientist yet he challenges nothing about organised religion and his mixtures of water and garden herbs do nothing but create a stagnant stench. They certainly have no evidence of healing properties. The man is completely deluded, he can't compete with William in that field or with any of us in what we achieve."

"William?"

"Withering. A fine doctor and a fine man too. He can treat heart disease with a foxglove. Quite a discovery wouldn't you say, but Hawke's concoctions are no more useful than using stale urine to treat a patient."

Jan thought it may be wise to guide the focus for Rosa/Samuel away from Silas Hawke as talking about the footman of Great Barr Hall clearly made the atmosphere very uncomfortable.

"I'd be interested to know what you and your learned friends are discussing this evening, Samuel?"

Unexpectedly, Galton in the body of Rosa became even more visibly distressed.

"We need to somehow stop these awful, awful happenings from occurring." Rosa placed her fist to her mouth and squeezed her eyes shut, clearly moved by something.

"What awful happenings?" pressed Jan.

"The gruesome deaths of these poor people. Not only is it terrible for the victims and their families but it also threatens to put a stain on this area of Birmingham where we have otherwise explicitly raised the profile of success. Birmingham is now a city that is a world leader.

"Matthew and James have their factories here and they have created mass employment for the area. Matthew has even introduced the Assay office to firmly place us on the map of silver manufacture.

"We choose to live in the area too, we like it here, but scattered along the pathways and woodlands between Soho House and Great Barr Hall fresh bodies of the deceased are regularly being discovered. Bodies ripped to shreds, limbs torn from their bodies and randomly scattered about. Facial features missing. It is unclear if this is the work of a man or an animal. Or dare I say it a mixture of both. That's what it seems to be anyway considering the appalling way that the bodies are being mutilated and dismembered."

Sounds like the work of a werewolf, thought Judd.

Rosa sat forward and faced Jan to address him directly. This was very unusual for someone under hypnosis. The body language of how she sat was more akin to being masculine though than that portrayed by a female. "Allow me to elaborate. You may think that it is I who is the mad man for what I am about to convey to you, but we know that in France, Bavaria and Austria the werewolf has stalked human prey."

Bloody hell, Galton thinks it too, thought Judd. It comforted him to learn that his theory obviously wasn't too wacky and wasn't only attributed to him.

Galton in the body of Rosa continued. "We now fear we have the same curse here in Birmingham. If we industrialists are half as knowledgeable and philanthropic as we like to think we are, then it must be up to us to save this community. We need to destroy the werewolf before it kills again."

Judd swiftly concluded that the skeleton that had been found in the ruins of Great Barr Hall could not have been the only victim to have met an untimely death at this particular time.

He also recalled what Dr Keeley had told him about the markings on the skeleton and how they had most likely been caused by a canine type creature due to the 'V' shapes in the bones.

This was chilling stuff.

The scandal had obviously been kept quiet at the time. No matter how visionary and capable the members of the Lunar Society undoubtedly had been, there was no technologically enabled news media back then to highlight this pattern of disturbing deaths. And the Lunar Society had the authority and know how to be able to bury bad news.

But what on earth was the story behind the body in Great Barr Hall? Did the Lunarticks bury the body in the house in order to hide its secret all these years? But surely, they would have known it would have been discovered one day, even centuries later, which would undoubtedly place a slur on their great work. Why would they want to risk that?

These men weren't stupid, they had been a unique collective of the most brilliant minds that had ever lived. They would have known that they were shaping history with their industrial achievements and that they were leaving an unrivalled legacy.

And why only hide a single body when there had clearly been more that had seemingly met the criteria to be hidden?

It was more likely that the other victims had been traditionally buried in local graves, just as any other dead person would have been no matter how they had died. Once back in England, Judd planned to take a wander in the graveyards of north Birmingham, starting with St Margaret's Church in Chapel Lane, Great Barr for an indication of any untimely and violent deaths.

So, what had set that one body apart to have needed to have been buried in secret within the fabric of Great Barr Hall?

For now, it remained a mystery, but Judd concluded that the skeleton that had been discovered in Great Barr Hall must have been hidden without the knowledge of the Lunar Society.

But why?

CHAPTER 27
IN MY LIFE

Finally, Judd underwent his own past life regression.

"The digital recording of your regression is all part of the service," explained Jan. "Usually I just provide the client with a memory stick and as a back-up email the recording as an attachment, then leave them to listen in their own time. However, I'd like to play this back to you while we are still together, Mr Stone."

"Ok."

"It was quite remarkable," said Rosa, who was enjoying a much-needed cup of coffee following her own notable regression and then witnessing Judd's.

"I know it was," said Judd. "That's one thing I didn't realise would happen. I can actually remember the whole experience."

"Past life regression is a form of mild hypnosis which teases out the hidden memories of past incarnations that are buried in the subconscious mind," explained Jan. "That means they are always there but need a helping hand to surface. Why? Because we are so preoccupied with our current life and the associated priorities and involvements that they become buried."

"It's amazing stuff. I mean Rosa, you were a gunmaker seemingly on the pursuit of a werewolf, and then I discovered that I was a gunslinger in the wild west!"

"You know in spite of why most people want to undergo a past life regression, and believe me a good few can end up disappointed when their expectations aren't fully realised, it is rare for people to discover that they were once someone famous in a past life. Usually they never even knew a prominent historical figure of any kind. But Judd, to find out that you had rubbed shoulders with both Billy the Kid and Doc Holliday in the wild west - well that was something special," said Jan.

"Well, I guess it explains my liking for the booze and gambling."

"Have a listen again from this point."

On the playback, Judd's accent could be heard switching seamlessly from Brummie to an American Southern States accent.

As the true story unfolded, Judd revealed that his name back then had been Flint 'Ace' Monroe. His time had largely been spent frequenting saloon bars where he had taken full advantage of the saloon girls on offer and indulged in hours upon hours of boozy card games – earning him the nickname 'Ace' – along with his speedy ability to draw a gun. He was also an above average piano player and often spontaneously tinkled the ivories in the saloons, prompting a mass sing-a-long.

John Henry 'Doc' Holliday had been plagued with tuberculosis which eventually claimed his life on 8 November 1887 and before that Billy the Kid had been fatally shot on 14 July 1881, aged just twenty-one. Flint 'Ace' Monroe had been killed a year earlier in 1880 by a gunshot wound to the head. He had been shot from behind in a cowardly act which meant that Judd in his regression had been unable to articulate who *his* killer had been.

There would have been no shortage of suspects for killing 'Ace' as he had attracted many enemies due to his flamboyant lifestyle and the circles in which he had chosen to move in.

The year of the killing had not escaped Judd as he realised it had been exactly a century apart as to when his musical hero John Lennon had been gunned down in a similar way.

Judd, as Monroe, had spoken about the bouts of coughing that had peppered the conversations that he and Doc had shared, as did many a slurred word for both of them (evident in Judd's regression) through the effects of regular alcoholic intake.

Val Kilmer's portrayal of Holliday in the film *Tombstone* had been one of Judd's favourite performances by an actor, and now he understood why he had always held such a fascinating interest for Kilmer's expert unfurling of the colourful character of the gunfighting dentist.

Ace's time on earth had been cut short with his murder, which unfortunately prevented any insight into the thirty second shoot out that became famously known as the gunfight at the OK Corral. However, the regression had still been able to reveal many tales of violent and regular saloon bar brawls and even the odd gun fight that had not seemingly been historically documented.

Maybe if 'Ace' had taken up Doc's offer to leave Las Vegas with him to join the lawman Wyatt Earp in Arizona, instead of staying put, 'Ace' may have lived a longer life?

But perhaps tapestries of lives are meant to be woven in the way that they are interlaced – because if 'Ace' had lived differently and for a longer period that would have prevented Judd's incarnations and experiences being played out the way they were meant to be thereafter.

Besides 'Ace' felt right at home in the evolving city of sin amongst the prostitution and gambling. He had even silently been involved in the construction of the Doc Holliday Saloon which had been erected in 1879, not long after he had helped silence a certain Mike Gordon who had turned nasty in a saloon recklessly firing bullets all around him. Gordon had taken exception to a saloon girl who had refused to leave town with him. Not long after, he had been found dead with his death shrouded in mystery, but fingers were being firmly pointed at 'Doc' Holliday and 'Ace' Monroe.

Monroe's time with Billy The Kid had been nowhere near as entwined as it had been with 'Doc' Holliday, but he had stood side by side with the outlaw during a bar brawl. The new found friends had been picked on because of their youthful and seemingly vulnerable appearances. This had been a clear mistake by the aggressors, as William H. Bonney, as Billy had introduced himself to 'Ace' only hours earlier, and Monroe emerged as the undoubted victors of the fight.

Bottles had been smashed over heads but fortunately there had been no need to draw guns on this occasion – which probably prevented the tale finding its way into Wild West history. Whereas, Billy The Kid's killing of a blacksmith in similar circumstances had helped cement his notoriety.

Judd had been able to identify with the gambling and drinking parallels with his current existence but he hadn't been as keen to note the similarities to his own violent bar brawls over the years. And not to mention the similarity of fighting in the days of youth when a young Judd Stone had been a bonafide football hooligan.

Once the accounts of Flint 'Ace' Monroe had been articulated via the digital recording, Jan paused the transmission.

"So, Judd, having died in 1880 in the shell of Flint 'Ace' Monroe, as I explained, other lives are not nearly as remarkable or associated with fame. After your passing as Ace you were soon reborn into your next life but it seems the little boy you became led a fairly unremarkable life."

"Are you kidding me, Jan?" exclaimed Judd excitedly.

"As little Alfie I was witness to the first ever goal scored in the football league! That's just awesome to know that I did that."

Jan was surprised at Judd's assessment. "Oh, ok, that's great. I'm glad your next life after being a wild west gunslinger pleases you."

So, through his regression, it became evident that Judd had by this time seemingly surfaced in his beloved West Midlands area. He had been one of the two-thousand five hundred spectators present to watch Wolverhampton Wanderers play Aston Villa at Dudley Road, Wolverhampton on 8 September 1888. This match was the first match ever to have been played in the English Football league. This 1888-1889 season had been the only one where Wolverhampton Wanderers, or Wolves as they are also known, had hosted their opponents away from the famous Molineux Stadium.

Judd, as little Alfie, had been able to describe the noisy and excitable atmosphere amongst the working-class spectators as they entered the stadium and wrestled for their viewing positions. Alfie's father had worked in the iron foundry on the morning of 8 September and after a minimal engagement with soap and water and a quick bite to eat, he had walked his son through the smoggy streets of the Black Country, filled with industrial smoke and related smells, to the Dudley Road standing area where they had mingled with the rest of the gathering crowd.

Alfie's father placed his young son on his shoulders so that he could get a good view of the football taking place on the muddy pitch. His father had managed to maintain his footing on the slippery boards, which at least prevented the soles of his hobnail boots sinking into the sodden turf below the wooden platform. His son hadn't missed any of the action, including when Aston Villa full-back Gershom Cox put the heavy ball into his own goal (not net as there weren't any yet!) to give Wolves the lead. The match eventually ended a draw at 1-1.

Within a short amount of passing years there had obviously been quite differing experiences for Judd in his previous lives. Wild west gunslinger Flint 'Ace' Monroe on one side of the Atlantic Ocean, followed by young Alfie Burford, an innocent football mad kid living his life in England's manufacturing heartland of the Midlands.

It was a sad irony that in the childhood of his current life, Judd had never experienced the same love and affection from a loving father that young Alfie had enjoyed. This fact wasn't lost on Judd.

Jan spoke again. "And as you had originally requested, Judd, we were able to go even further back in time and connect with the period of the Industrial Revolution, in particular the window of 1750 to 1850."

"Yes, I was some posh bloke living in London it would seem. I'm glad my West Midlands working class roots began to take hold once I became Alfie."

"But as a private detective there were some traits that chimed, Judd," interjected Rosa. "You were willing to offer a £100 reward for the capture of the London Monster. That was one hell of a sum of money for the time."

"Yes, the London Monster. How crazy was that guy, going around the streets of London sticking pins and needles in women?" said Judd.

During the full scope of the regression, Jan had guided Judd back to his former life as John Julius Angerstein, a merchant of German parentage actually born in St Petersburg, Russia but who had moved to London at the tender age of fifteen.

"I've just looked you up on my phone's search engine," said Rosa. "You were famous enough to have a place in history, Judd. It also says here that there is an Angerstein Lane in Greenwich and even a public house named after you."

"Well that part's very fitting, the pub bit," smiled Judd. "Remind me of the years I was on earth as this chap again,

Rosa."

"1735 to 1823. You also had a substantial collection of fine art it says here, with most of your collection ending up in the National Gallery in Trafalgar Square and The Louvre in Paris."

"Well that explains why my eye caught sight of your paintings doesn't it?"

"I'm not sure I can compete with the Rembrandts, Turners, Rubens and Raphaels that Angerstein collected."

"Nonsense. Don't hide your light, girl."

"Thanks. At least I have one fan, huh?"

"You'd better believe it. Can you do something for me please, Rosa?"

"Sure."

"Will you search through my hair at the back of my head please?"

"What?"

"Please."

"You're still weird."

"I'm fascinated to discover if something is there."

Rosa got up from her chair and began to separate strands of Judd's locks to reveal random patches of skin. The touch of Rosa's fingers caused a nice sensation in Judd's stomach and tickled at his scalp.

"What am I looking for, 666 the mark of the beast?" asked Rosa.

"No, you cheeky mare. But I am after a mark of sorts. Like a birth mark, but not a number."

Suddenly Rosa stopped for a moment. "Hold on, what's this?" Then she started at Judd's hair again, intensifying her hair separating technique. "Wait, there is something. Yes, a red mark. Definitely. Your scalp is a different colour in this particular spot."

"I'm not surprised."

"Neither am I," offered Jan.

"What is all this?" asked a puzzled Rosa.

Jan provided the answer. "Birthmarks often exist as

tell-tale signs of how we may have exited our previous lives."

"Oh, I see. I get it," said Rosa. "Judd had been shot in the head when he was Flint 'Ace' Monroe, the cowboy."

"Exactly," said Judd.

"Wow, that's pretty mind boggling. And what's more you can clearly see how traits from previous lives take shape in current existences. Our regressions have thrown up some telling stuff for both of us, Judd."

"That's true enough," said Judd. "But one thing is for sure where I'm concerned."

"What's that?"

"Unlike you, if I was Angerstein during that particular period of time then there is no way that I was ever one of the jigsaw pieces that fitted the Lunar Society."

CHAPTER 28
A DAY IN THE LIFE

With Gia Talia and company on their way to Prague to assist with the 'disappearance' of Rosa, she and Judd needed to stay an extra night in the Bohemian city. That situation wasn't exactly inconvenient for either of them, few people could ever find a stay in Prague unpleasurable.

Fortunately, Rosa and Judd had discovered that they actually liked one another's company and they had made the most of things as if they had been friends for years.

Together, they sampled more of the locally brewed beer and other distilled alcohol and took in a small number of Prague's wonderful sights such as the Strahov Monastery and a closer inspection of the medieval astronomical clock. It hadn't been lost on Judd how the latter had obviously undergone an amazing feat of engineering that mirrored many of the innovative achievements of the Lunar Society, perhaps even outperforming the efforts of the Lunartick clock maker John Whitehurst. Nor the fact that the clock actually incorporated the moon's developing shape of the lunar phase via its silver and black transitions.

But all of that came much later as Judd found that he had enough time on his side to have liaised with Sandy back home via a very pleading telephone call.

He had managed to get Sandy, and Jan for that matter, to agree to participating in a very ambitious past life regression under very exceptional circumstances.

Judd, Rosa and Jan were sitting in Jan's place with the laptop screen facing them, whilst following Judd's guidance, Sandy had set up a network of laptops in the hall where the FIGHT meetings usually took place.

"Ok, let's check the connection first," said Judd. "Can you guys in Birmingham see us on the screen from over here in Prague?"

"Put it this way, I can see your ugly face," replied Errol.

"Hey, Errol, how are you mate?" said Judd.

"All good in the hood."

"Cool. Hi Sandy?"

"Hello again, Judd."

"Thanks for rounding these reprobates up at such short notice, Sandy."

"It was a pleasure, although I'm a little nervous about all of this."

"It'll be fine," said Judd.

"Here, who are you calling a reprobate," shouted Kingsley.

Judd laughed. "You know I'm only joking. I love you all really. Anyway. Jan meet Sandy, Sandy meet Jan."

"Hi Sandy."

"Hi Jan. I look forward to working with you. I think."

"Same here."

Judd addressed both sets of people at opposite sides of Europe via the technological connection. "Ok everyone, just to be clear and to highlight what I have discussed with Sandy and Jan. As you are aware the past life regressions that have been encountered amongst us have firmly taken us back in time to the gatherings of the Lunar Society. Well, things have now evolved even further on that score since I've met Miss Van Hendrix here in Prague. Jovanna has discovered during her regression with Jan that she was once Samuel Galton, yet another member of the Lunar Society."

"Hello everyone," said Rosa. She and Judd had agreed beforehand that it made no sense to reveal her true identity to the gathering in Birmingham.

Echoes of 'Hello' and 'Hi Jovanna' came across the airwaves from Birmingham.

"I know it's a bit ambitious but Sandy and Jan are going to attempt to perform simultaneous regressions with you all and take you all back to the times of the Lunar Society. I'm really keen to try and understand what happened to that poor girl who seemed to have met her fate in Great Barr Hall all those years ago and I think this is our best chance."

"And what about you, big man?" asked Errol. "You've been dodging your regression for some time now."

Jan offered some assistance on Judd's behalf. "I have regressed Judd back to the said period and he was not connected in any shape or form to the Lunar Society."

"It's true," said Judd. "I was a chap called Angerstein living in London at that time so there's no point me taking part in this err, experiment."

"Damn, I was running a book on you definitely being Matthew Boulton," said Slim.

"Yippee. What a result," piped up Maureen. "That means you owe me a few bob, Slim."

"You lot are unbelievable," said Sandy. "You're supposed to be moving away from gambling and here I find you betting on the potential past lives of Judd."

"Sorry Sandy," said Slim like a naughty schoolboy. "It just seemed like a bit of harmless fun and a good idea."

"You are recovering addicts, Slim. Gambling can no longer ever be considered as harmless fun or a good idea for any of you," chastised Sandy.

"Anyway," said Judd, keen to get things back on track.

"I'm not Matthew Bouton and I don't know who is or who was. For now, if he has an incarnation in this life it remains a mystery. Now are there any questions before we begin?"

"No questions Judd, and I really hope this works for you," said Sandy. "But I'm not used to undertaking such a grand scale of past life regressions or connecting with others via technology."

"I have to declare, me neither," said Jan.

"I know this is a bit unprecedented both, and if it doesn't work at least we tried," offered Judd. "I won't be blaming either of you if it proves unproductive, ok?"

"Ok," Jan gave a thumbs up. "Good luck, Sandy. I don't envy you; you have a lot more folk to deal with than me in all of this."

"Thanks Jan. I think luck is something both of us may need. Ok, Judd. We'll give it a go," said Sandy.

"I'm very grateful to you both and everyone willing to take part. Sandy, Jan over to you."

It was a mammoth undertaking but patiently and collectively with a mutual display of impressive expertise, Jan and Sandy managed to take everyone down the staircase of past years to arrive at a gathering of the Lunar Society. Judd looked on in awe.

Through the voices of their past lives, the FIGHT members and Rosa began to tell a remarkable true story. All except Kenny who slept like a baby through the entire unveiling:

A collection of Lunar Society members were in the garden area of Heathfield House, home of James Watt, hardly able to believe what they were witnessing.

"He's gone mad," said James Keir (Aki).

"It's as if he's become another person altogether, he's like a rabid animal," interjected John Whitehurst (Niko).

"Or a werewolf," said James Watt (Errol), the owner of Heathfield House.

Silas Hawkes, the gentile but deluded footman, had

indeed taken on a seemingly new persona. He had fresh blood around his mouth and was snarling, just like a dog. Or a wolf.

"Well it is a full moon," said Josiah Wedgwood (Maureen). "But surely, there can't really be such a thing?"

Terror was in all of their voices.

"Do you think the girl is dead?" asked Erasmus Darwin (Kingsley).

"We need to get close enough to be able to tell for sure, but the poor thing looks it from here," offered William Withering (Abdul). "I believe that Hawkes is having a reaction to the potions that he has been making. He has been collecting all sorts of mushrooms believing that he can mix them to cure illnesses of the mind, but I fear that this is the ironic results of his product that we see before us. I had warned him to be careful but he had threatened to kill me if I persisted to interfere with his work."

"Do we know who the girl is?" asked Wedgwood.

"I recognise her as a local girl. I believe she offers herself for money if you know what I mean," said Watt. "I think she goes by the name of Ada. I don't believe she has any family. Poor child. It seems this monster had more on his mind than simply intercourse."

Silas Hawkes gave a loud growl. He had the dead girl at his feet and was being cornered by chairs and sticks, much like a lion in a circus might be, as the learned men desperately attempted to control the situation.

Suddenly he was able to grab a waving stick from the hands of William Murdoch (Skye). Hawkes tossed it like a javelin, and the distance in which it travelled to where it eventually ended up, underlined the amount of strength that the man suddenly seemed to possess. Next, Skye let out a painful yelp as she recalled Hawkes' hand connecting with Murdoch's chin sending him straight to the ground.

James Keir (Aki) made a move towards the out-of-control footman but the table simply splintered across his back just like in the modern-day movies, quite a feat for chairs of once such astonishing and sturdy craftsmanship. This wasn't lost on the clockmaker John Whitehurst who would one day become the polish carpenter Niko. "Th... that's not possible."

Hawkes turned on a sixpence and came face to face with the closest Lunartick to him who had been Richard Lovell Edgeworth (Wanda). "He's going to kill me," screamed Wanda as the grip from Hawke's hand came around the inventor's throat.

The creature-like-man loosened his grip once Erasmus Darwin had struck him over the head with a branch that he had stumbled across, but it had little effect except to annoy Hawkes even further. Lovell Edgeworth dropped to the floor grateful that his life had been spared as he clung at his aching throat but it didn't look as if Erasmus Darwin was going to be so lucky. Hawkes snarled and drooled before physically leaping in the air just like a wolf.

Darwin closed his eyes waiting for the undoubted sealing of his fate, but suddenly a loud crack could be heard and Hawkes fell to the ground. Darwin opened his eyes to see a pool of blood flowing from the chest of the footman.

"I...is he dead?"

"I think so," said Murdoch who had just managed to get to his feet although a little groggy. "It looks like you got him straight through the heart."

"Well you took your time," said James Watt. "We almost lost Erasmus there and I don't think this madman would have stopped until we were all dead."

Samuel Galton (Rosa) walked towards them with a smoking gun, flanked either side by Joseph Priestley (Slim) and Matthew Boulton (his incarnation in the twenty-first century still currently unknown). Boulton had no speaking part in the playing out of this story between modern-day Birmingham and Prague but the others confirmed that his presence had been there all those years ago.

"He's dead alright," said Galton. "Matthew here made sure that I had a silver bullet to fire, complete with a Birmingham Assay anchor hallmark no less. He handed it to me to place into my gun while we enjoyed a beer or two at the Gunmakers Arms. A werewolf can't survive a silver bullet. He's dead, and it's only fitting that I shot him considering I introduced him to you all."

"He's no more a werewolf than I am," spluttered Withering. "This is murder. He may be a mad inventor but he is still a man."

"Really? And should I have just left him to kill our friend, Erasmus here then? Is that what you would have preferred, Withering?" retorted Galton.

"No, of course not," conceded Withering. "I accept that you had little choice."

"And one thing that I'm sure that we will all agree on," interjected Priestley. "Whether Silas Hawkes was a man or creature, or both, he is clearly responsible for the brutal killings that have been occurring in and around this area."

The Lunar Society members all took turns in looking at one another and there were unanimous nods of the head.

"This can never be explained," said James Watt. "Most folks in these parts would never be able to comprehend the scale of these tragic events and this... this... unprecedented conclusion. No one can ever find out about what has happened here."

"Agreed. We will have to get rid of the bodies," said Priestley.

"I pulled the trigger, I should suffer any consequences," offered Galton.

"Not a chance," said Darwin, who was now breathing a little better. "You saved my life and we all agree that either one of us would have pulled that trigger if we had been in your position. We are all in this together, right gentlemen?"

Again, all those present offered affirmations.

"And another thing," said Priestley. "We now know that the killing will stop."

"This is true," said Withering, now identifying more easily with the reasoning of his friends.

Galton suddenly developed a forlorn expression on his face. "This monster must have surely killed my scullery maid, Martha. She's been missing for months but where is the poor girl's body?"

"Perhaps she just left Brummagem for some reason. We can't be sure that she has been killed," said Murdoch in a Scottish accent.

"We agreed to refer to this wondrous place as Birmingham," said James Watt.

"This is no time to be pedantic, my friend," said Galton.

"You are correct, Samuel. Forgive me."

"Nothing to forgive," replied Galton. "I hope Martha did get away but I fear the worst for her. It's just a hunch I have. Anyway, we need to think about putting these bodies that are most definitely before us to rest."

"I know of a few spots around this land that would suit a burial," offered Watt. "There are enough of us to dig the graves and have this horrible episode over by sunlight."

"No time like the present," said Darwin.

"Wait," said Galton. "There are also enough of us to take these bodies another two miles or so. I know the very place. At least allow me to reduce the burden on James of having dead bodies buried about his property. I doubt knowing that their corpses were rotting nearby would do much to diminish any of your bouts of anxiety and depression, James. And like I said, I feel an air of responsibility for getting you all mixed up in this. Yes, it's definitely the best option. A watery grave awaits these two and it reduces the risk of them ever being discovered. We can follow the light of the moon. Do we all agree?"

Again, they all agreed.

CHAPTER 29
GET BACK

The next day Rosa was forever facilitated out of harm's way courtesy of the particular set of skills of Gia Talia and company.

Similarly, Sab and Yasmin had successfully shepherded Ravesa safely onto a plane back to Romania, complete with change of hair colouring and a fake passport. The two sisters had nursed her back to good health in the safe haven of the Rotunda and had even gotten her through the cold turkey period to come off drugs. Of course, nobody was so naïve that they failed to realise that Ravesa still had a long and winding road ahead of her. She would most likely experience bouts of depression and some post traumatic flashbacks, but she was undoubtedly now in a much better place both physically and mentally than she had been in more recent times.

Ravesa had made two short phone calls before leaving Birmingham. The first to her worried but soon to be overjoyed mother which resulted in widespread delight in the knowledge that the whole family would be waiting with open arms at Bucharest Otopeni airport to welcome her safely home. The second call was to Judd Stone simply to say thank you.

Yet, for all of Judd's feelings of deep-rooted guilt that he had held over the years for his perception that he had time and time again let down the women in his life, both Rosa and Ravesa would forever hold a great deal of immeasurable gratitude for Judd Stone. Typically, and perhaps tragically, their appreciation in the huge part that he had played in helping them to escape the unsavoury lives that they had been forced into was pretty much completely lost on him. This, even after both women had explicitly conveyed their thanks to him.

Just two days after Ravesa had left England, Judd's departing plane from Prague touched down in the very same Birmingham airport that had enabled her to return to the safety of her family.

Judd waited patiently to leave the plane, being one of the remaining few to grab his hand luggage from the overhead locker and bid farewell to the cabin crew. As he placed his right sneaker onto the steps that had been temporarily attached to the aircraft, Judd simultaneously switched his mobile phone from the safe-flight mode. The signal reconnected as Judd walked across the tarmac of BHX and as soon as it had, he received a very unexpected and distressing call from Errol.

"Sandy, I came as soon as I heard. How are you?"

Sandy was lying in the intensive care unit of Birmingham's Queen Elizabeth Hospital resembling something of an ancient mummy. It broke Judd's heart to see so many bandages wrapped around her head.

"Hello, Judd. Apparently, I'm lucky to be alive, but I don't feel very lucky if I'm being honest. I'm going to need cosmetic surgery due to the bite marks on my face and I'll never have a natural left earlobe again. At least they have told me that my spleen and kidneys will heal in time, I guess that I am lucky that there is no permanent damage there." Sandy began to cry.

"Hey, it's ok Sandy. Don't cry. Who did this to you?"

"I don't want to say. I haven't even told the police."

"Why the hell not?"

"I just want it all to go away. I can't stomach a lengthy court case, going through all that anxiety. Besides I don't want to face any repercussions, I may not be so lucky next time."

"So, you do know who your attacker is?"

Sandy didn't answer.

Then Judd remembered the time when Vina had bitten off the ear of a thug when they had gotten into a fight with a street gang. Biting the face and ears was not a widely used trademark of attack or defence for most people. Therefore, Judd realised that the attack on Sandy had potentially been an attack by Vina. And in light of more recent discoveries he also knew that the psycho bitch was well capable of such a thing.

"It was Vina, wasn't it?"

"How do you know?" asked Sandy. Typical of the integrity of this sweet woman, she may have wanted to stay silent, but equally she couldn't lie to Judd now that he had hit the nail on the head.

"I just know. I've seen what she's capable of. What happened?"

Sandy looked down through her swollen eyes and took a deep breath. "She came for a routine past-life regression. You know, she always seemed such a sweet girl. Well perhaps she still is, after all it was her past carnation that attacked me. At least I think it was. It's another reason I don't want to tell the police. I don't think she could help it."

"Don't make excuses for her, Sandy You have always told me that the regressor remains in control."

"To be honest it is appropriate that I tell you, Judd. It has all fell into place now. It all fits."

"What do you mean? What all fits?"

"You know. After all that has been happening with the group's regressions and the Lunar Society. Especially following the other night when we all discovered the mystery of those killings that happened so long ago in and around Great Barr."

"Go on."

"When I took Vina back to that time period, like we had done so often before during her regressions, she experienced her usual feelings of pain and claustrophobia, but this time she took on a persona filled with rage. Judd, she was snarling like a dog and then suddenly, totally unexpected, she just leapt at me. I don't remember much else after that, I blacked out with my own pain soon after. Her attack was ferocious."

"You poor thing, Sandy. You didn't deserve that. Does that mean she must have left your place still being in a state of her past-life regression?"

"It's possible but I doubt it. Before I blacked out, as an attempt to calm her, I quickly tried to bring her out of her regression back to her current life. At one point I actually asked her, 'Vina is that you?'"

"And then what?"

"She smiled and said coldly, 'It sure is, Sandy.'"

"And still she continued and left you for dead. That's even worse. The fucking bitch, I'll kill her."

"No Judd, no more violence. Please."

Judd realised that he needed to contain his anger so not to distress Sandy any further. "Ok, ok Sandy. I promise. Please, don't upset yourself. But, just to be clear we are concluding the same thoughts here aren't we?"

"That Vina was Silas Hawkes in a previous life?"

"Yes," said Judd.

"It seems more than likely."

Then Judd remembered Vina's birthmark. It was positioned exactly where the silver bullet would have hit from Samuel Galton's (Rosa's) smoking gun.

Things certainly were falling into place.

CHAPTER 30
HEY BULLDOG

"Hello Harper."

"Come in, Judd. She's waiting for you in the spare bedroom. She must be mad wanting to see you again but I guess she must have her reasons."

Judd crossed the threshold of Harper's house and ventured up the stairs eager to see his wife.

As he cleared two steps at a time in order to hasten the ascent, Harper shouted after him. "Turn right on the landing and it's the second door on the left."

Within seconds Judd was in the bedroom that Brooke was now using as her home. She was sitting at the dressing table with her back to him. She seemed to be looking at the screen of a laptop.

Judd soon found himself beside her. He shortly became confused though; it was clear she was still being frosty with him and she hadn't even bothered to turn and acknowledge his presence.

So why had she called him over? Then his heart sank as he noticed the memory stick poking from the USB port. *Oh no*, he thought. *Had even more unsavoury footage of him found its way to her?*

"Hey, Brooke. I came as quickly as I could, it was nice to hear your voice at the end of the phone."

Now she turned to him but she didn't break into a smile. "I need to show you something, Judd."

"Look, Brooke. What's the point of torturing yourself with any film you may have of me? I know I've done wrong but believe me, no-one is punishing me for that as much as I am myself."

"What are you talking about? Not everything is about you, you know, Judd. Get over yourself for a minute, will you? What I have to show you goes far beyond your sordid little rendezvous. This is serious. Really serious."

Judd was beyond intrigued. "What is it?"

"Pull up that chair so you can see the screen. But listen carefully, this changes nothing between you and me. Ok?"

Judd nodded; his optimism shattered to pieces.

"But no matter how much of a dick you are, Judd, I also know how good you are at fighting crime and seeking justice."

"Well you certainly have my attention, Brooke. What are we looking at then?" Judd could see that Brooke had opened a list of icons on the screen, any of them poised to be clicked into and accessed.

"Remember the day of the shooting?" said Brooke.

"How could I forget? I lost two of my best friends on that day and the love of my life was put in a coma for months."

"The love of your life whom you cheated on… Anyway, let's not get into all that, right now. On the day of the shooting, William gave me a jiffy bag. I thought it rather strange so I asked him about it and he said that it was just something that I may need to give to you someday. He described it as being a bit of insurance."

"Really, what was in the bag?"

"This memory stick that is sticking out of the laptop. I put it in my handbag when we were near the canals and forgot all about it until now. It obviously remained unseen during all the time I was unconscious, but today for some reason, I remembered that I had it and so I decided to take a look. What I found was mind boggling to be honest Judd, and it seems that what William and Crystal were looking into was extremely dangerous."

"Dangerous enough to get shot by a motorcycle assassin, huh?"

"I fear so. I guess you and me were just collateral damage."

"So, what's on the stick?"

"All kinds of documents, transcripts, records, photos. There are even just some rough notes of William's and Crystal's on here – to be honest with you there really is a plethora of information. Let me start with this. Have you ever heard of Pavlov's dogs?"

"No, I don't think so."

"I've heard of it before. The stuff about Pavlov is no secret, it's all over the public domain. I remember a teacher at school even telling us about it. But the story of Pavlov's dogs is just the context behind the more disturbing stuff we're going to look at on this memory stick. It's the evolution beyond his experiments that are more alarming and clearly they were meant to have been kept secret."

"Go on," encouraged Judd.

"Well, William and Crystal had saved some PDF versions of Pavlov's work. Ivan Pavlov was around in the 1890s and early twentieth century but his publications have since been reproduced for e-reading and are available on various internet sites. I think William and Crystal used his findings as a starting point for their research."

"So, what were Pavlov's findings with our canine friends?"

"He was an experimental psychologist, in particular he studied classical conditioning."

"Classical conditioning. What's that exactly?"

"Well it was no surprise that a dog would salivate when it was fed, but Pavlov discovered that the dog could also salivate if it connected something totally different to the food itself. At first the drooling reaction developed when the dogs simply caught sight of the white coat of the lab technicians. The dogs worked out that food was on its way as the technician was the one who provided them with food, so they began to salivate before they had even set eyes on the pieces of meat that they were being fed. The white coat became the trigger for salivation."

"Ok, that makes sense."

"So, then this Russian dude, Pavlov began to experiment with the possibility of other triggers. He introduced metronomes and the ringing of bells for instance, and sure enough the dogs connected these sounds with the act of being fed causing them to salivate even when the food never came."

"So, the dog's brains became conditioned to salivate as it connected with these sounds? Its behaviour mirrored as it would when simply eating meat, even when no food was present."

"Correct. Meat is the natural stimulus. When meat is placed in front of the dog it'll naturally salivate. Ordinarily a ringing bell has no connection for the dog to salivate, but over time, once the dog learns that a ringing bell equates to the possibility of it getting a meal the sound of the bell becomes what is known as a conditioned stimulus."

"Oh wow, I can see how that could happen. There's no reason why this couldn't progress to conditioning human behaviour right?"

"Right. It's the research into that possibility which I believe may have caused harm to our friends."

Judd had to agree. "You know, William once told me how minds can be controlled. It was fascinating stuff. He was such a clever man. Coupled with what he told me and just my own feeble research into mind control programmes such as MK Ultra, I totally get that triggers can be put in place to control behaviour, including human behaviour. The book *The Catcher in the Rye* for example is believed by some investigators to have triggered John Lennon's killer into action. And to this day, Sirhan Bishara Sirhan swears blind that he has no memory of firing the gun that assassinated Bobby Kennedy. He states that he was taken into a darkened room at the Ambassador Hotel where a mysterious woman wearing a polka dot dress planted a hypnotic signal to trigger the killing."

"Well believe it or not, Judd, I have actually seen reference to that and more in some of these documents held on the memory stick."

Judd took a deep breath and rubbed his hand across his stubbled-face, preparing himself for whatever else Brooke was to reveal to him. There would no doubt be some relief in understanding what sat at the heart of the death of his two friends, but it also wasn't lost on him just what a very distressing experience it was likely to be.

Brooke continued. "I have been able to identify from the information scattered around this memory stick that William and Crystal had indeed made the connection of using conditioned stimulus to control human behaviour. The problem is they had case studies on a vast range of people and it's highly likely that they were never meant to have had knowledge of such information."

"So, it could have been someone named in the case studies who killed William and Crystal because they were pissed off at being scrutinised without their consent, perhaps?"

"Unfortunately, but I think it's even more sinister than that, Judd. I doubt that the people in the studies even know that they are on anybody's file, let alone this memory stick. I suspect that William and Crystal were not the only ones who have information on these individuals and it's more likely that the damage was done for our two friends when they crossed a line."

"What line?"

"I think that they must have sourced this information through computer hacking and somehow they got found out. Either that or they got caught undergoing some kind of unauthorised surveillance."

"So basically, someone didn't like them snooping around and sticking their nose into their business?"

"I fear so. I think they got into something far deeper than they should have and unfortunately they messed with some very dangerous characters."

Judd took another deep breath and he recalled the discussion that he had had with Gia. She had also remarked how William was getting in above his head and she had tried to warn him off. When a gangster warns you off because those people that you're fucking with are even more dangerous than they are, it signifies something colossal in terms of danger.

"So just what exactly did William and Crystal discover that was bad enough to have their lives cut short?" enquired Judd.

"It seems that these people that are mentioned in the files were able to be controlled by having their obsessions, fears or vulnerabilities manipulated."

"What do you mean, Brooke?"

"Well it seems that anything that is highly relevant to a particular person can be utilised to reach into the gates of their mind and produce a mechanism for controlling them. Let's take you as an example, Judd."

"Me?"

"Just hypothetically speaking. Don't worry, I couldn't see a specific file on you."

"Glad to hear it."

"But, let's just say if these mind controllers would want to get to you, Judd, your obsession may be identified as The Beatles. Therefore, one of their songs could become the trigger to prompt you into action. They would find a way to plant the tune into your head and condition you to act on hearing the song. Other ways to control your behaviour could be through your vulnerabilities, and I'm not having a go here by the way, honestly, but maybe a pack of cards or a roulette wheel could become your trigger as you are vulnerable when it comes to gambling. It could even be the presence of a certain woman or women."

Judd looked sharply at his wife.

"Like I said, I'm not having a go, I'm just illustrating a point," said Brooke.

"Ok, I get it."

"Having a relevant trigger for a person perhaps makes the job of controlling and conditioning a lot easier to implement."

"I think it would, most definitely."

"There's evidence in here of individuals being controlled to commit murder, and yes including assassination and professional hits. Other crimes that have been orchestrated by conditioning include theft, fraud, trafficking drugs and even trafficking humans. When you think about it how many young girls go into prostitution or porn to fuel a drug habit? Pimps and unscrupulous sex industry workers can control those women based purely on their vulnerability. It is easy to control their behaviour as the presence of a man's dick can be the conditioned stimulus for a shoot of heroin."

"I guess you're not wrong there, Brooke."

Brooke opened up a file from the computer's list view. "There's evidence here of one guy being threatened with the death of his family. He lost his parents when he was young and so now, he has this deep-rooted fear of losing his kids and it's tormented him at the deepest core of his mind. When he receives a text message or a phone call telling him that his kids are about to be killed, in order to prevent it happening he 'blindly' goes out and commits armed robbery. He drops the money somewhere for the instigators to collect but here's the thing, he wakes up never knowing that he was ever involved in the criminal act. There are pictures and videos of his kids on the file."

"He's been brainwashed and conditioned by having his fear manipulated. The threat of his family's demise serves as a trigger for irrational behaviour."

"Yes exactly. But I also discovered something very sad, Judd."

"Go on."

"We both know William and Crystal would only have used any of these techniques for good, right?"

"Of course. Their overriding passion was to try and find a cure for multiple sclerosis."

"Ok, we both knew that. It seems that they didn't find a cure for MS but they did find a way to perhaps control it."

"Really?"

"Yep. It looks like they still had work to do but they were making one hell of a progress with William's symptoms. Look at this particular case study, Judd." Brooke opened up a new file and the photograph of a familiar face sat above the words on the opening page.

"It's William. He had a case study on himself the old fox," said Judd.

"Yes, and wait until you read it. Let me warn you, it'll break your heart, Judd."

Judd leant nearer to the screen of the laptop in order to scan the text.

"May I?" he asked.

"Go ahead."

Judd took control of the mouse from Brooke so that he could scroll through the many pages of the case study. After a few minutes digesting most of the text, he sat back in his chair in wonder at the amazing work of his dead friend and his wife, Crystal – who had been playing no small part in developments at all it would seem.

"So that explains why he was able to walk on that day along the city canals," said Judd. "I thought it strange that he was relying less and less on his wheelchair but never thought to question it. I was just thankful that he seemed to be coping." Judd turned to Brooke and he could see that she had tears trickling down her cheeks.

"Crystal was his obsession," said Brooke wiping away a tear. "She was his life, love and constant companion so the two of them were trying to condition his mind to override the symptoms of MS by using Crystal as his conditioned stimulus. When you think about it it's a perfect solution. Perfect and beautiful."

"It's amazing and makes perfect sense. She was always by his side. But as they were trying to use that sense of stimulus conditioning linked to personal relevance for the good of William and potentially other sufferers of MS, there are obviously others who wanted to use such techniques for evil. The assassinations, the killings, the prostitution, the trafficking etcetera."

"And as I've demonstrated, sometimes these despicable acts are being committed by decent humans that are helpless because they are being controlled. Their behaviours are being controlled by a conditioned stimulus."

Judd shook his head in angry disappointment that human beings could be used and abused in such a manner. "And those at the root of the control, the ones who are orchestrating it all, they are the true benefactors whilst never being in danger of getting caught themselves. They're untouchable."

"Untouchable and only void of the danger of being found out until William and Crystal stumbled upon their practices."

Judd leaned forward. "And looking at some of the names I can see on file these people pulling the strings are operating internationally?"

"I can confirm that, Judd. There are all nations in here. This is a global major crime organisation. Do you think it is the Illuminati?"

"It could be, many believe that they secretly control

most things. Or something even bigger if that's possible. With maniacs like that running people's lives it's no wonder William and Crystal were killed if they were on to them. You must give me the memory stick Brooke; I don't want anything coming back on you for any of this."

"I don't want anything coming back on you either, Judd."

"I knew you still loved me."

Brooke narrowed her eyes.

"Ok, sorry. Bad joke."

"I want to show you this one last file before we decide what to do with all of this, Judd. It's for a Croatian motorcycle enthusiast who is living on a council estate in England. He owns a late 1990s 100cc motorbike, it's all he can afford. However, there are times when he leaves his flat and his modest motorbike has been replaced by a Harley Davidson or equally impressive piece of machinery. And when such an impressive motorcycle is waiting for him in his parking space, he becomes a professional hitman. I think he killed William and Crystal. They had him on file and they never even knew that he was coming for them."

"Open up the file, please, Brooke. I want to see his picture."

Brooke did as was asked and Blago Vitez stood next to a Harley Davidson, smiling and clasping a helmet decorated with flames either side of its shell.

CHAPTER 31
OH! DARLING

Judd pressed send after crafting his text: *call me unsophisticated but this classical stuff really doesn't float my boat quite like Lennon and McCartney can.*

The reply from Sab came back almost instantly: *You're unsophisticated.* Judd smiled. He had asked for that.

He had waited patiently in the shadows of Birmingham Symphony Hall's stage door for Vina Moreno to appear following her latest performance in the orchestra. Finally, she arrived.

"Hello, Vina."

"J…Judd, how are you?" Vina was startled by Judd's sudden appearance but soon broke into a smile. "I take it that you came to watch the show." This final comment sent Vina into a typical deluded sense that all was forgiven and Judd had come to woo her again.

Judd realised that he really was dealing with a proverbial bunny boiler. "Why have you been avoiding my calls, Vina? I think we need to catch up over a coffee, don't you? Don't worry, it's my treat." The uncompromising tone in Judd's voice, coupled with his stern stare, brought Vina a little closer back down to earth. She knew that he would be well aware that she had sent their 'sex tape' to Brooke hence her deliberate avoidance of him lately.

But surely, he couldn't possibly know what she had done to Sandy? There was no way that the regressionist could have survived that attack, and even if she had, she should have been much too scared to blab. No, Sandy must have died. Vina knew that she had done a good job on her. And she had already kidded herself that there would be no good reason to point the finger at her, such was the reflection of her narcissism and the weird wiring of her thought processes. Vina quickly pushed any more thoughts on that score from her head.

"Look, let's go back inside. We can discuss things in the dressing room. It'll be clear by now. I think what we have to talk about may be better done in private. I can see you're angry with me, Judd."

Judd's expression held firm. "After you."

As Vina swiveled on her heels with her back to Judd, he didn't notice her swiftly grab the phone from her pocket and punch in a quick text, her torso shielding the activity. She nodded to a security guard who nodded back before giving Judd a stare which didn't perturb Judd in the slightest. Before long they had ventured down the corridors and were inside the now empty dressing room.

Vina appeared to close the door behind her but in truth she had left it accessible by sneakily placing down the latch. She manoeuvred around the room before finally resting on the back of a chair. She looked as seductive and as beautiful as ever but Judd had no interest in going there again.

"Why did you do it, Vina?"

"Do what?"

"Send Brooke your little home movie?"

"I didn't."

"Don't insult my intelligence," snapped Judd. The

raising of his voice caused Vina to flinch.

Suddenly Judd's phone pinged from inside his pocket.

"Sound like someone wants you, Judd?"

"I'll take a look later. I'm kinda busy right now. Now talk."

"Ok, ok. You hurt me, Judd. And you used me. I thought we meant something to one another and then you go and dump me as soon as your as good as dead wife wakes from her slumber."

"Don't talk about her like that. Anyway, what did you expect, Vina? I never promised you anything. I never once indicated that we had a future together. It was fun but no more than that. Besides, why on earth would I hook up permanently with a psycho like you? In truth I wish I'd never met you, Vina."

Vina sensed that Judd's hostility was down to more than the damaging communication with Brooke.

"You've found Rosa, haven't you?"

"I may have done."

"Well until you return her to me you won't see your money, Judd."

"Return her to you? You must be mad? Oh, wait, I forgot for a moment. You are fucking mad."

"Our agreement was that you would never speak to her. You were meant to simply locate her and let me know where I can find her."

"Well that would have suited you just fine, I'm sure, but sorry, I did speak with her and didn't I learn a hell of a lot about you, Vina Moreno?"

"It's all lies. She is vulnerable and confused. That's why I needed her to be found but not approached. So that I can make her safe and look after her."

"You make her safe? Don't make me laugh, Vina. You are one nasty piece of work and I've made sure that you can never harm her again. She's safe now but only because I'm ensuring that she never has to see you again."

Vina was incensed. "You bastard. Who the hell are you

to play fucking God? You really don't know what you've done do you, Judd?"

"Oh, I think I do."

"You stupid man, it's not just me that you will have upset if we never see Rosa again. You're in big danger now, Judd. You may think you're a hard man but you have just got yourself into something that is way over your head."

"I'll take my chances. I'd rather die knowing that I have made that poor girl safe than hand her over to you and whatever you're fucking involved in, you sick bitch."

But even though he knew what Vina could be capable of Judd still managed to underestimate her poker face as she gave no indication that someone had crept into the room behind him. He lost consciousness as soon as he was clubbed over the head.

As Judd came round, he was almost knocked unconscious again as a punch connected with his right cheek. He spat out the blood and looked through swollen and squinting eyes to see two figures stood before him. He recognised them both. One was the security guard who Vina had acknowledged when re-entering the Symphony Hall but the other's presence was a little more surprising. It was the huge Dutchman, Larz.

"Do you have to hit his face?" said Vina from somewhere in the background. "His face is much too handsome to be ruined, boys."

Straight after Vina had delivered her words the security guard punched Judd in the stomach which considerably winded him. "Is that better, Vina?" asked the security guard.

"Yes, take note Larz."

Larz snapped at Vina. "Don't tell me what to do, Vina. I'm only here to find out what happened to Rosa. I think this bastard must have killed her. The fact that I've discovered that you have him all packaged up for me is just an unexpected bonus." Larz turned his full attention to Judd. "You fucking lied to me." The Dutchman struck Judd hard across his other cheek.

Judd was unable to fight back. His wrists had been tied with chains above his head astride some kind of pipe and his legs had been taped together. The chains had been slackened enough so that his feet could touch the floor making him an ideal version of a human punch bag.

"Now tell me, Stone. Where is she?" demanded Larz.

Judd made a whisper.

"What's that I can't hear you, speak up you piece of dog shit."

Judd's head hung low. Again, his voice barely reached a decibel.

"How can he speak when you've half killed him, Larz," said Vina. "You really haven't mastered the art of torture, have you? Typically, you steam straight in like the tonto you have always been and fuck things up."

"Fuck you, Vina."

Larz leant into Judd to jeer him. "Now, what did you say, cowboy? Huh, come on spit it out."

"Judd raised his head and said perfectly clearly: "I said, you hit like a fucking girl," and with these words Judd delivered the most powerful headbutt of his life straight onto Larz's nose.

"He's broke my fucking nose. Again. The bastard."

Vina walked over from the shadows and stood in front of Judd, which allowed him some temporary respite by blocking the path of his attackers. Even so, she was mindful enough not to stand too close to Judd so that he couldn't reach her with a headbutt as he had done with Larz.

"Look, Judd, baby. You need to make this a lot easier on yourself. Just tell us where Rosa is and all of this will be over."

"If I tell you, you'll have me killed anyway."

"It's true that if you've spoken to Rosa you may have

been told things that I and others didn't want you to hear, but I still have the power to save you, Judd. You need to start trusting me again."

"How could you do that to your own cousin, Vina? You really have no boundaries, do you?"

"I knew she could make me money and she owed me."

"She owed you nothing, you were just jealous of her. You have been your whole life. Tell me, did you have her mind fucked with too?"

Vina was slightly taken aback at Judd's change of questioning. "What do you know about that?"

"Enough, but that's all I'm saying."

"I didn't fuck with her mind, if you have spoken with her, you'll know that. She's still family at the end of the day but like I said she could make me money. I made sure she was one of the lucky ones."

"Yeah, she's really lucky to have a cousin like you." Even in these circumstances, Judd was able to maintain his sarcasm.

"What else do you know about us?" asked the security guard.

Judd laughed. "So, you're one of this gang of warped fucks too, are you? Except you only think you are. You're just a fucking puppet doing the dirty work for those that bask in the splendour. You're being used you stupid prick. You and many like you, you fucking Neanderthal."

The security guard managed to manoeuvre himself to reach around Vina's position and he connected with Judd's ribs. Although Judd was hurt, he managed a mocking laugh.

Vina pulled out her mobile phone. "I have someone who wants to speak with you, Judd."

Vina messed with the screen and the keyboard of her phone and soon established a video link connection to a man with greased back hair and a leathery face. She held the screen up for Judd to see.

"Hello Mr Stone." He spoke with a New York accent.

"Who the fuck are you?" asked Judd.

"That's not important. What is important is that you've been compromising our European operation of trafficking and pimping out girls. I'm told there are at least two of our girls that you have made disappear. Now I want to know where they are and I want to know what else you fucking know about us?"

"All I know is what you've just said. You pimp out girls. Big deal, it happens all over the world."

"Yes, it does, but we do things, how shall I say, a little differently and I think you know that Mr Stone."

"I don't know what you're talking about, and what's more I don't fucking care."

"Oh really? You see I think you do. Cast your mind back Mr Stone, assuming it's still functioning after your recent beating. Do you remember a guy by the name of Ocran La Bouef?"

Although he felt weary, Judd was shocked into being more attentive once he had heard the name.

"Oh, I can see that I now have your attention, Mr Stone. You see Mr La Bouef was an acquaintance of ours. We shared similar goals in life and through some research that I've had undertaken I understand that you knew of him too. The strange thing is that he disappeared. Poof!...into thin air it would seem, just like that. Now that's a bit of a coincidence wouldn't you say that your name is linked with Ocran and now two of our girls are also fucking missing. That makes you a major fucking pain in the ass, Mr Stone."

Ocran Le Bouef had been the slimy record producer of Phoenix Easter. Judd had secretly killed and disposed of his body after discovering that he had planned to have Phoenix killed. Judd thought that he had done enough to cover his tracks and he knew he had made sure that the body would never be discovered, but it made sense now that Le Bouef could have been part of this recently discovered dangerous set up of extreme global organised crime.

"I have no idea what happened to Le Bouef. Why would I?"

"I don't believe in coincidences Mr Stone without a clear linkage, that's why. I guess we should have done a better job of getting rid of you when we got rid of your little friends hey?"

Judd suddenly became angry. "You killed William and Crystal?"

"Well not me personally, but I helped orchestrate their demise. You see, you fucking limeys just can't keep your nose out of other people's business. And when you snoop where you're not meant to be snooping there are consequences to be had. And when someone actually has the audacity to fuck with us then again there are consequences to be had, aren't there Larz?"

Larz looked puzzled, not expecting to be addressed. "Huh?"

"Kill him," came the order from the psychopathic American.

Judd closed his eyes waiting for a bullet to enter his skull. In a twist of irony, it seemed that Larz had been ordered to fire the fatal shot.

Judd heard the gun fire and his life flashed before him. This was weird, he didn't feel any pain.

A couple of seconds passed and he slowly opened one eye. Judd was shocked to see Larz lying in a pool of blood with the security guard standing above him holding a smoking gun.

The American at the end of the phone spoke again. "You see, that's the kind of thing that can happen when you fuck with us, Mr Stone. Larz here thought he could take one of our girls away from us and then just swan back in when it suited him. No fucking way."

"You're just a bunch of fucking nutters."

"I beg to differ Mr Stone. If that were the case, you'd be dead by now. You see, while you are holding information then you have some mild use to me alive, for the time being at least. So, I'm going to let Don the security guard here continue to torture you until you sing like a fucking canary. But note this, Mr Stone, I am not known for my patience. Eventually we will kill you if you fail to tell us what we want to hear. So, it's up to you my friend. You can have a long period of suffering like you have never experienced before, which could result in an eventual painful death depending on your own personal pain threshold and resilience, or, you can simply tell us what we want to know and I may consider letting you walk free, under certain lifetime restrictions of course."

"You'll kill me anyway whether I talk or not. I'm not fucking stupid. If I'm going to die anyway, I'll do it on my own terms and I ain't telling you shit."

"That Mr Stone is a gamble you will just have to take."

"Tell me. Who are you and your little outfit? The Illuminati?"

The American laughed loudly. "Everyone calls us that, people's imagination can be so muted. In reality we just exist like the air and like a cloud. We are untouchable so we prefer not to have a label. That way we exist but there can be no trace to us whatsoever. The likes of you will never know exactly who we are but that doesn't mean that you don't know something and you knowing just a fraction of what we do is just a bit too uncomfortable. So, like I said, I'll look forward to Don here finding out just what you do know."

"And like I said, I ain't telling you shit."

"Goodbye, Mr Stone."

The screen fizzled out. Vina spoke next. "Please babe, just tell Don and Blago what you know."

"Blago?"

Just then a motorcycle could be heard revving outside the basement door of the Symphony Hall. Judd surmised that there was a tradesman's entrance or the like nearby. Soon after, the engine ceased to make a sound and Blago appeared with his flame decorated crash helmet perched under his arm. He made his way over to Don and Vina and stood beside them. He had the audacity to smile sarcastically at Judd.

Judd's anger was almost tangible. He tried to break free to reach the motorcyclist but his efforts were futile. "You killed my friends and put my wife in hospital you fucking scum." Then Judd remembered what he had read on the information held on the memory stick. He couldn't help but be angry at what Blago had done but he thought about the possibility of him being brainwashed and conditioned to kill when provided with a snazzy motorcycle as the trigger.

"What bike have you come on today, Blago?" asked Vina.

"Ahh, just my old 100cc Honda, Vina."

Judd was confused.

"Blago has been so effective in what he does he has actually agreed to work for us," said Vina. "We pay him well."

Fuck. Blago was now on the payroll, realised Judd. The hitman's eyes had now been opened to the terrible killings that he had done and yet he was obviously totally ok with it.

Strangely, Judd now realising that Blago was a bonafide organised crime member gave him some comfort. He now knew that when the time came to avenge the deaths of his friends, he would be killing a murderer who was fully aware of his actions.

Vina continued to talk. "I'm going to leave you with these two boys now, Judd. I simply can't bear to watch."

"You're a fucking warped bitch, Vina. You are truly fucked in the head; do you know that?"

"You should show me more gratitude, Judd. If it wasn't for my insistence, you'd be dead by now. It was me that made sure that you at least have a chance. Please baby, just tell them what you know. Where is Rosa and where is

Ravesa. Just tell us and I swear you'll be set free."

"How do I know that for sure?"

"Because I have told them that I don't want my child to be born without knowing who his father is."

Judd could hardly process Vina's words. "What the fuck are you talking about?"

"I'm pregnant, Judd. Tell them what you know and you will get to see your child being born. If you don't you won't. It's as simple as that, lover. It's up to you. I can have you taken down from these chains right now if you want. All you have to do is say that you will be with me. Come on Judd, listen to what I'm offering. Be with me and I can stop this right now. Join me and our child and they will let you live."

CHAPTER 32
HAPPINESS IS A WARM GUN

Judd's answer had been 'No', perhaps missing a golden opportunity to at least be free from the chains around his wrists which could have enabled him to think again regarding an escape. But it was the weight of the metaphorical chains of any kind of relationship with Vina that prompted his answer. He couldn't commit to Vina's offer even for a second or in jest.

He also hoped against hope that she had been lying about the pregnancy.

As soon as he watched Vina's wiggling backside walk away from him and leave the basement, even now looking as attractive as ever, he felt the butt of the gun connect with his head courtesy of Don. Blago then followed that strike with a kick to Judd's balls.

"This is going to be so much fun," said the Croatian motorcycle enthusiast.

"It certainly is," said Don as he tucked the gun in his trouser waist and punched Judd in the stomach once again.

"You're a pair of fucking pussies," said Judd who was struck again by each of them for his insolence.

"I don't reckon this piece of shit will talk you know," said Blago.

"He's a stubborn fucker all right," answered Don.

"Maybe we need to get a little smarter with our methods of torture."

"What do you have in mind, Blago?"

Even though Judd was being held up by chains, he had only just realised that his wrists had actually been connected to the metal links with rope, it had obviously been an easier way for his captors to secure his wrists. He wondered if the knots in the rope would slip and loosen if he were to pull his arms downwards.

"I'll be right back," said Blago. "I think I have the very thing within the holdall on the back of my motorcycle."

As Don watched Blago walk away from the scene, the security guard cackled out of his toothless grin. He had taken his eyes off Judd just long enough for Judd to lift his legs and in midair create just enough gap between his taped legs to slot Don's head through them. Instantly, Judd began to crush Don's neck. As he squeezed, Judd was able to see that Blago was none the wiser as he left the room.

Don reached his hands up to Judd's legs to try and release Judd's grip but his legs were like a vice. Judd locked his legs in the same way a determined pit bull might lock his bite on any unfortunate victim.

Don turned red in the face as he frantically reached for his gun but he dropped it as he panicked, barely able to breathe. Judd squeezed his knees together tighter and tighter and before long Don lost consciousness. Judd wasn't sure if the security guard was dead or simply unconscious so he didn't know how much time he had to orchestrate anything else.

Judd pulled at the rope and he came to realise that the tussle had loosened the knots a little. He dangled his legs off the floor to see if the gravity of his weight would loosen the knots even further. Unfortunately, it didn't and

Blago re-entered the room carrying a blow torch.

"You cheeky bastard," he shouted as he saw his accomplice lying on the floor and he hastened his step to move swiftly towards Judd. "I used to use this for soldering copper pipes but today I'm going to use it to solder you, pretty boy."

Judd snarled with bravado but inside he was unusually worried. Here he was about to be tortured by a sick bastard with a blow torch and if Don was to wake up, he knew the gun was well in his reach too.

Blago flicked a switch on the blow torch and the flame ignited into life. "You know, the last time I used this on someone they actually passed out before I could even finish the job on them. I wasn't even able to tell if they could still feel their skin blistering and disappearing as I moved the flame over their body. It took a bit of the fun out of proceedings if I'm being honest, but somehow, I think you'll be different, tough guy. I think I'll hear you screaming right up until the point your heart eventually stops beating and gives up with the pain.

"You see, unlike the others I don't really give a shit if you tell me what you know or not. I just like torturing people like you. But if you do want a chance of staying alive, the smartest thing for you to do is to tell me where the girls are and what else you have discovered about the powers that be. Our invisible masters, shall we say. But I reckon that you're as stupid as you are brave ain't ya Stone? I think you'd prefer to let me kill you rather than you reveal anything, you stubborn and noble bastard."

"Eat shit and die."

"Ok it's your choice, hero. I'd like to say that this is going to hurt me more than it'll hurt you, but I don't like to tell lies." Blago moved the blowtorch towards Judd's face and danced it around close to his skin. He was teasing him for now. Judd could feel the heat on his cheek and even in his eyeballs.

Blago pulled the blow torch away. "Anything you want

to tell me?"

"Not in a million years you fucking prick."

"Ok, have it your way then." Blago moved the torch towards Judd's bare forearm. The pain was instant and excruciating but Judd refused to provide any satisfaction to his torturer. Judd gritted his teeth and didn't make a sound.

Then suddenly a loud bang echoed through the acoustics of the basement and Judd saw the blowtorch drop to the floor. Unlike Judd, Blago screamed with pain as he stared disbelievingly at the hole in his bloody hand. Blago turned around to try and grasp an understanding of what was happening and in doing so he took another shot in the chest killing him instantly.

"Sab, am I glad to see you," said Judd.

"You know, I had a hunch something was up when you didn't respond to my last text, which was me offering to treat you to a coffee. I was seeing Yasmin at the Rotunda and I knew you were close by at the symphony hall."

"I was kind of unable to get to my phone, Sab."

"So I can see. Those knots look pretty tight, let's see if this thing can burn through rope." Sab picked up the blowtorch and set to work. Judd's arms were soon free although they felt as if they were no longer attached to his body as they had been hanging in the air for so long. Sab was able to remove the tape with her hands and it was in the nick of time. Judd noticed Don start to stir and reach for the gun. With his arms near useless, Judd was able to kick the gun away and then stamp full force on the security guard's throat. Then he applied all of his weight onto his right foot until Don was dead.

"So, Sab. We have three dead guys here, two by gunshot wounds and another with a crushed windpipe. Do you think we can make this look like these three killed one another?" asked Judd with a wry smile.

"Easy. They'll think the security guard came down here

and stumbled upon these other two dorks who were up to some kind of mischief. We'll rearrange a couple of things and basically, we were never here, Judd. Now how about I treat you to that coffee...once we have seen to that arm, that is. Boy, it looks painful, I think you need to go to a hospital to be honest, Judd."

"Nah, the arm is fine. I'd rather not draw attention to it. I think I need something a little stronger than coffee though, mate. Let me pop to the gents, I'll run the tap over my arm, clean the blood out of this hair and then we'll go for a beer."

CHAPTER 33
WITH A LITTLE HELP FROM MY FRIENDS

"Cheers," said Judd clinking his glass on Sab's.

"Cheers. Well that was just like old times."

"What, you bailing out my arse? I think it was the other way around most of the time as I recall," smiled Judd.

"Fair enough, I particularly remember when that psycho killer Banks had me in his sights and you rescued me. You were just like my knight in shining armour."

"Now you're taking the piss."

Sab smiled. "No, seriously, I guess I owed you one, partner."

"Well thanks again, Sab. I didn't fancy being turned into fried chicken."

"How's your arm?"

"Not too bad. Looks like it'll heal. Thanks to you the heat wasn't on it for too long."

"That's good."

"Where did you learn to shoot like that?"

"Living in the States tends to make sure that certain things rub off on you."

"Of course. My next question is, so you carry a gun now?"

"Only for self-defence, or bailing out my old pals when they are tied up under a stage."

"Point taken."

"Besides, I knew that we were fucking with some dangerous criminals."

Judd frowned. "We?"

"What do you think I've been doing while you've been galivanting across Europe? I told you I'd be looking into things. It also turned out that my previous drawing of blanks in the US was only a temporary situation. It's just that things were, and still are really, so well hidden. Including within layer upon layer of corruption. That's why progress had been so slow."

"Had?"

"When I came over here, I told you that I kept a couple of cops deployed on the case over there."

"I remember."

"Well, it included a really determined pal of mine who continued to look into things for me. He was a good kid. He did a bit more than keeping his ear to the ground."

"*Was* a good kid?"

"Detective Arnold Briggs, better known to his friends like me as 'Arnie' was found floating in an LA swimming pool."

"Shit, that's rough. Could it have been an accident?"

"It was no accident; he was found with the shape of a diamond carved into his back."

"A diamond?" enquired Judd.

"Yeah, but I knew what it meant. The warning signs along the roadsides in America are displayed in the shape of a diamond. It was a warning to back off. Poor Arnie left behind a wife and two kids. I feel pretty terrible about it."

"Did he get any information to you, Sab. Before he died?"

"Yes, the kid did exceptionally well. They killed him

but the bastards were too late. Arnie got word to me the name of a kingpin in all of this, or someone who liked to think he was anyhow. We discovered that this whole worldwide crime organisation thing did include America after all. Thanks to Arnie, we came across a guy who pulled a lot of strings in the States, trafficking, drugs, killings, you name it this guy orchestrated it."

"Let me guess. Leathery faced guy, slicked back hair, baggy eyes, New York accent?"

"That's him, how did you know?"

"I had the pleasure of speaking to him not too long-ago over video chat. Turned out, he was instrumental in ordering the hit on William and Crystal."

The enormity of that knowledge wasn't lost on Sab's facial expression. "Really? The bastard. How do you know this?"

"He told me. Listen Sab, I need to bring you up to speed with some information held on a memory stick. William passed it onto Brooke the day he and Crystal were killed."

"Ok. I'm listening."

"It explains a lot more about all of this. Our friends uncovered some incredible things through their research, in more ways than one. The trouble is, after speaking with old leather-face it seems a lot of this criminal organisation, or whatever you call them, are untouchable."

"Well you'll be glad to know that Gabriel Bolan, Mr Leather Face himself, isn't as untouchable as he would like to think he is."

"How do you mean?"

"Think of this global outfit as a huge cake with layers upon layers of criminals. The ones who sit at the very top are indeed untouchable. In truth, the likes of me and you will never know who they are, Judd. Bolan is relatively important but he can be reached, he pulls many strings for sure but he's not an ultimate puppet master. Let's say he sits just above the jammy filling in this metaphorical cake but he sure ain't the icing on it."

"Ok, I get it," said Judd. "Wait a minute. If he can be reached let's hunt the bastard down and I'll kick him into next week. I'll make sure that his death is very slow and painful for him."

"Hold your horses, cowboy. Tomorrow he'll be opening a letter addressed to him sealed with a kiss. Only the kiss will be the kiss of death, the ricin will kill him within three days – so his death will be pretty slow and painful. The LAPD didn't take kindly to one of their own being killed in that manner. As you can expect though, killing someone like Bolan, considering the circles he moves in, couldn't be executed too obviously. There could be no open display of LAPD coming for Bolan as that would have upset those in the outfit that have certain members of the police in their pocket. Hence the ricin."

"I just wish I could have looked that scum in the eye myself and made him pay for what he did to our friends."

"We haven't done too bad partner, considering who we are dealing with here."

Judd took a swig of his beer to take the time to help process this latest knowledge. "You're right, Sab. Those who we knew to be involved are dead. I'm glad you put a bullet in that scumbag, Blago too. It's you who has done well, Sab. William would have been proud of you."

"Thanks, I hope so," Sab began to get a little emotional and wiped a tear from her eye.

"Sorry, Sab. I didn't mean to upset you."

"It's ok, I can still get a bit teary thinking of him and Crystal. I'm just relieved that we have managed to avenge their deaths. I think I'm crying due to the enormous sense of relief as much as anything."

"Does Ben know any of this?" asked Judd.

"Do you think he'd really buy into this theory of layers upon layers of untouchables?"

Judd smiled as he thought of their conformist friend. "No, it would blow his mind wouldn't it?" Ben Francis was an extremely efficient and well-meaning Detective Superintendent, but one that rarely thought outside of the box.

"We'll find a way to tell him it's all over," said Sab.

"Ok. Anyway, like I said, William would have been proud of you. And so, would Crystal come to that. There is still one person walking free though who has a lot to answer for."

"Who's that?"

"Vina Moreno."

CHAPTER 34
TWO OF US

Judd had been kidnapped again but this time he was strapped tightly to a chair. This was an ironic development considering that it was an approach that Judd had often taken himself whenever he had chosen to kidnap and torture someone.

Gabriel Bolan was standing over him. He was a larger man than Judd had imagined following his only previous encounter with him via a head shot on a telephone screen.

"You limey piece of shit," spat the American as he slapped Judd hard across the face.

"You hit like a girl," mocked Judd.

Standing to the side of Bolan was Vina. "You really do need to co-operate, Judd. I've told you already that I don't want this baby born not knowing his father."

"Do you really think I'd hook up with a bunny boiler like you, Vina?"

"We come as a package. If you want to see your child then you need to be with me. There is no other option, but if you don't tell us what we want to know then you won't be able to be with anyone ever again. You won't get away from us a second time."

Judd then looked to the left of Bolan and there stood Larz. He couldn't believe it. How could this be? He had been sure that the beefy Dutchman had been killed. He and Sab had agreed that no loose ends could be left before they had exited the basement of the Symphony Hall.

And come to think of it how was Bolan here? Had he managed to dodge his ricin infested mail?

Judd couldn't remember how he had got here either. He had no recollection of being struck over the head like the previous occasion that he'd been tied up.

Larz passed Bolan a towel and he placed it over Judd's face. "Hold still you limey son of a bitch."

Judd could hardly breathe as the material covered his face. Bolan was stretching it tightly and Judd could do little to resist as his hands had been robustly secured.

The cotton towel soon became wet and Judd realised that he had fallen victim to the technique of waterboarding. He found it increasingly difficult to breathe but he tried not to panic as the cold dampness consumed his face. He knew that the idea was to drive him into such a panic that once the soaking material was removed, and he gasped for air, he would be expected to talk.

And that's exactly what happened next.

"Well, Stone. What d'ya know," snarled Bolan.

"Plenty but nothing that you'll ever hear you leathery-faced prick."

The towel came over Judd's face once more. It felt even colder and the gush of water that came next felt ten times more forceful than the initial downpour.

In fact, somewhat uncharacteristically, Judd was now beginning to panic. It seemed that the force of the wetness just kept coming. It felt relentless. It would only take one act of mistiming their withdrawal of the towel and water for it to result in Judd not being able to breathe altogether.

Or perhaps they were now simply planning to kill him anyway…

Judd was now beginning to feel a weight on his torso in addition to the waterboarding.

"No, no stop…. stop," he cried. "Stop, stop."

Wait. How was he able to talk? Wouldn't the towel and water prevent him from speaking?

But his face felt so wet.

Then, Judd opened his eyes to find Mr Mustard licking his face affectionately.

Judd had dreamed the whole episode and his faithful dog had woken him from the horrible experience.

"Hey, Muzzy. Love you boy."

Mr Mustard continued to wag his tail and lick his owner's face with increasing excitement.

"Ok, ok I'm pleased to see you too. No doubt you want your breakfast."

The dog jumped energetically off both his owner and the bed and ran into the kitchen eager to get his feed.

In contrast, Judd slumbered out of bed, stretched and hitched up his lounge pants. He followed the bounding Mr Mustard into the kitchen, opened a tin of dog food and dropped it in to the dog's bowl. As Mr Mustard devoured the foul-smelling meal, Judd filled his kettle with water and set it in motion to boil for a much-needed mug of morning coffee.

As he watched the steam escape from the spout, Judd found himself thinking about the prospect of being a father.

Judd had almost become a dad once before, but that chance had been taken away from him in the cruelest of ways when his first wife, Frankie, had been murdered along with the unborn child that rested inside her.

It was fair to say that he hadn't expected such a development with Vina, but the more that he reflected on the situation, the more he actually realised that he wasn't totally against the idea of becoming a dad– even though the news had initially come as a huge shock.

But there was one major overriding problem. The

expectant mother was a psycho. Any onward relationship with Vina, even if she would allow a relationship to unfold at a distance, which was unlikely, would always be problematic.

As if Vina would ever allow things to run smoothly anyway and surely whatever else she was criminally involved in was going to have a huge impact too. Plus, how on earth could having a kid with this woman ever lead to a much-wanted reconciliation with Brooke?

Since marrying Brooke, he had assumed that they would have children together at some point, but now perhaps that ship had sailed?

So, was the toxic bunny-boiler Vina now his only chance of having a kid?

But what if the kid had their mother's genes? Or his for that matter. Judd wasn't naïve, he knew that he had been no saint over the years, in spite of his good heart. This kid could turn out to be a right vicious handful.

Judd also doubted his ability to be a good father, he tended to fuck everything else up in life so why should fatherhood be any different?

Judd turned to his friend. "What a fucking mess, Muzzy. "What should I do, boy?"

Mr Mustard broke away from his food and looked at his master with unconditional affection.

"Come on boy, I need you to learn to talk. I need some good advice because at the moment all I can seem to understand is that I'm well and truly fucked." Mr Mustard cocked his head to listen, as dogs often do, while Judd spoke to him.

The kettle finished boiling and he poured the hot water into one of his Beatles mugs whilst adding two spoons of instant coffee and his habitual four sugars.

He opened the fridge door, grabbed the milk, took a whiff from the opening of the plastic bottle and concluded that it was just about fresh enough to use. He promptly added the creamy white liquid to the contents of the mug.

He knew he somehow needed to find Vina again.

Firstly, to work out the future of his child and secondly to bring her to justice. Just how both of these things could ever be a compatible act he was yet to fathom.

He collected his mug of coffee and wandered into the living room. The painting *If Above us is only sky, John must still walk amongst us* by Jovanna van Hendrix hung stylishly on the wall. The other painting that he had purchased in Amsterdam, *De privedetective,* had pride of place in his office instead. Judd figured that they had to be the best two paintings hanging on any of the walls in The Rotunda building.

He took a swig of his coffee and looked at the noble face of John Lennon looking back at him.

In a mock Liverpudlian accent, Judd addressed his musical hero. "And tell me, John. What would you do, if you were me?"

CHAPTER 35
SILVER LADY

"Thanks for accompanying me on my first day outdoors without crutches, Harper. I'm not confident enough to be out on my own just yet."

"What are sisters for?" replied Harper. "Besides, I've enjoyed our girlie day out together to be honest. We should do it more often. And anyway, I don't need my arm twisting for a spot of retail therapy."

Brooke smiled. "It's been nice. I can't believe I came across that silver letter opener too. I paid a bit more than I would have liked for it but I thought what the hell. For some reason I really connected with it. I just had to have it."

"What the hell indeed. After what you've been through you deserve to treat yourself, Sis. Let's have another look at it."

The two sisters paused walking for a moment and unlinked arms so that Brooke could pull out an antique silver box from her coat pocket. She opened it to reveal a silver blade being cushioned on a red velvet pad."

"It's beautiful," said Harper.

"It certainly is. I fell in love with it as soon as I laid eyes on it. I simply had to have it."

"And it's in perfect condition for its age."

"I think it was the ornate handle that really drew me to it. Look at the swirling decoration, Harper. The attention to detail is amazing. What an antique. I feel so lucky."

"It's gorgeous."

"At first, I thought it may have been made in Sheffield as so much steel and silver comes from those parts, but I was really pleased to discover the anchor engraved upon it. The fact that the item was made in Birmingham really put the icing on the cake."

"It's such a shame nobody sends letters anymore."

Brooke reflected on her sister's statement. "It is when you think about it. Although, Judd was never any good at sending me romantic love letters."

"Well that doesn't surprise me. That man's name and the word romantic cannot be used in the same sentence, Brooke. You're well rid of that useless prick."

Thinking of Judd served to alter Brooke's exuberant mood. "You know, Harper. Believe it or not he could have plenty of romance in him. He treated me like a princess most of the time. He was so gentle and kind, and I always felt so safe with him, you know, like he protected me."

Harper rolled her eyes. "Oh my God, you still love him, don't you?"

Brooke sighed and looked a little sad before replying to her sister. "Harper, I'll always love him. I hate him but I'll always love him."

"You were always too good for him."

Then suddenly Brooke's attention was drawn elsewhere. "Wait," she said.

"What?"

"I can't believe where we have stopped."

"Huh? We are standing outside some old community hall, that's all. It needs a lick of paint too I hasten to add."

"I think that this is the community hall that Judd

attends."

"What?"

"For his meetings."

"Meetings?"

"You know, for therapy, for his gambling.

"Yet another reason to dump the chump." Sensing what Brooke was keen to do next, Harper had to think on her feet, determined to get her sister away from there as quickly as possible. "Come on, let's go home. It's starting to get dark."

"I really should pop in, just in case he's there. It seems silly to walk past."

Harper tutted and rolled her eyes again. Subconsciously she spotted that there was a full moon in the sky. "Brooke, this is a bad idea."

"Please, Harper. Just five minutes. If he isn't there we can just leave again."

"Five minutes. No more."

"I love you, Sis."

"Yeah, yeah."

Brooke and Harper walked up the steps, pushed open some double-doors and soon found themselves in a room with a small number of eyes fixed upon them.

In the centre of the room, chairs had been placed in a circle but not all were yet occupied making it clear that the session hadn't quite started yet. Some people were still moving around the room and a few of them had cups of tea or coffee in their hands as they stood around chatting.

"Please, come in. Can I help you?" came a kind voice through the small sea of bodies. Of course, the welcoming voice had belonged to the sweet soul of Sandy.

"Oh, hello. Err, pardon me," replied Brooke feeling a little awkward. "I'm looking for Judd Stone."

"Judd. Do you know him?" asked Sandy.

"You could say that," answered Brooke.

"He should be here soon."

"This is the gambling therapy thing, right?"

"Yes, this is Fighting Gambling Together. We're called FIGHT for short."

"So, he does actually come here then? I wasn't convinced that he did."

"Who exactly are you?" enquired Sandy.

"Wait, I know who you are," came another voice. "You're Brooke, aren't you?" said Errol. "My, you are as pretty as he always said you were. He's told me a lot about you, Brooke."

"You're Judd's wife?" asked Sandy.

"Not for much longer," said Harper. "Come on Sis, he isn't here, let's go."

"You're welcome to sit down and have a coffee with us," offered Sandy.

"Erm, it's ok. I don't want to intrude. I can see you're about to start your session," answered Brooke.

"Shall I tell him you called?" asked Sandy.

"Erm, no it's ok. I was just passing. It was nice meeting you all."

The group all smiled and bid Brooke farewell. Then just as she and Harper turned to leave another figure burst through the doors.

Sandy's tone wasn't half as welcoming once she caught sight of this particular visitor. In fact, she seemed a little scared. "You're not welcome here, Vina." Sandy stood up and actually cowered behind her chair as if it could protect her somehow.

Brooke realised that she was now standing face to face with the woman who had been responsible for wrecking her marriage. The same woman who had had the audacity to sleep with her husband while she lay in a coma in a hospital bed. The same woman who had been so cruel that she had sent the barely revived Brooke an explicit video of her and Judd going at 'it' like rabbits.

Vina looked through Brooke as if she wasn't there. "I have come for a past life regression and I want it to be held in parallel with all of you. I think I'm close to knowing all the answers and it involves everyone in this room."

"You heard what Sandy said," said Errol. "You're not wanted here."

"You don't tell me what to do," spat Vina.

"And you can't come in here demanding all sorts," retorted Errol.

"You will all do as I say." There was a madness in Vina's eyes. She seemed almost feral in her mannerisms which totally belied her classy dress-sense.

"Well I'm telling you that you're not welcome here," said Brooke.

"And who the fuck are you?" barked Vina.

Harper stepped in in typical big sister fashion. "Who the fuck are you, bitch?" Then it clicked with her. "Wait Vina? No, you're kidding me. My brother-in-law actually put his dick in you?"

Vina finally snapped, her feral persona escalated and she leapt towards Harper grabbing her by the hair and wrestling her to the floor. Immediately her teeth began to bite at Harper's ear.

"Get this mad bitch off me," shouted Harper.

The whole of the group pretty much moved forward all at once to break up the assault, but Brooke being the nearest, coupled with having the most desire, got there first and she jumped on the back of Vina.

Brooke's intervention had worked and Vina turned her attention away from Harper and towards the wife of Judd Stone.

After she and Brooke had rolled on the floor for a moment, they both managed to stand up and square up to one another. Like a wild animal Vina broke the deadlock and pounced at Brooke.

Brooke managed to get a couple of punches in but the ferocity of Vina's attack meant they had little effect. Vina was snarling like a rabid dog and it was taking all of Brooke's strength to prevent Vina's teeth from connecting with her face.

It was Kenny who attempted to break up the fight first but amazingly Vina shrugged off his grasp with ease and knocked him to the floor. Kingsley tried next but he suffered the same fate.

Vina was like a woman who had been possessed. She was wild and out of control.

Brooke managed to get another punch into Vina's body but again it had little effect and now Brooke was close to losing her balance altogether. Her energy levels were also low as her recovery from being in hospital was still not totally complete.

In the meantime, Harper was still lying on the floor clutching at her bloody ear.

Maureen realised that desperate measures were required if they were to halt this manic assault and she smashed her tea cup over the head of Vina. But the Spanish cellist didn't even flinch as the crockery danced across the floor.

Vina now had Brooke around the throat and her hands were squeezing tighter and tighter by the millisecond. Brooke was struggling to remain conscious. The strength of Vina seemed out of this world.

Slim pitched his can of fizzy pop at Vina's head with impressive accuracy but the tin can just bounced off Vina's head causing a hissing spillage on the floor but nothing else.

Something had to be done to stop this crazy woman before she killed Brooke.

Abdul looked around for anything that could be used as a useful intervention to the attack. He spotted a houseplant. He rushed over to the pot, picked it up and smashed it over Vina's head. Soil and leaves spilled all over Vina's hair and shoulders but still she continued with her vicious assault on Brooke.

Then the next thing to connect with Vina's head was a book courtesy of Wanda, quickly followed by a kettle at the hands of Errol.

But still she continued to attack Brooke.

Skye ran over to the lamp that Sandy liked to use to create a warm atmosphere for the group. Incredibly, that too proved to be an ineffective weapon.

Everyone felt so helpless.

And then she stopped.

Vina released her grip on Brooke's neck and seemed to freeze like a statue.

What on earth had happened?

Had she suffered a heart attack? There had been such ferocity in her assault it wouldn't have been a surprise if this had been the case.

Then, as she slowly fell backwards away from Brooke, the blood stain below her left breast became clear.

Vina fell to the floor and all eyes fell on Brooke.

Brooke was standing over Vina's body holding the silver letter opener that she had purchased only hours before.

And now it had saved her life.

Everyone then looked around at the mess on the floor, finding it difficult to take in. There was broken pottery, a dented kettle, spilled soil, a damaged house plant and fizzy pop flooding out of a can. A book also lay close by, its pages concertinaing from its overturned spine. A lamp lay smashed beyond repair.

The sequence of events had been symbolic yet the connection was never made.

Those who had attempted to intervene had each taken something to use against Vina that had been perfectly aligned to their previous lives in the Lunar Society.

The pioneer of steam, James Watt had struck a kettle over Vina's head courtesy of Errol. The botanist William Withering, these days known as Abdul, had chosen a plant pot as his weapon of choice.

Slim, who had once been Joseph Priestley had used a fizzy drink can, quite fitting considering that it had been Priestley who had invented carbonated drinks.

Maureen had used a tea cup. Okay it hadn't quite been a stunning piece of Wedgwood pottery, but it had been a form of pottery none the less.

Wanda who had once published many books as Richard Lovell Edgeworth had struck a tome over the attacker's head.

And Skye Collins, formerly known as William Murdoch, the inventor of the gas light and who in Persia had believed to have been the incarnation of Marduk, the ancient god of light had raced to use a lamp as her weapon of choice.

But in spite of all of these symbolic efforts, it had been the silver of Birmingham that had finally halted the attack, courtesy of Brooke's recently purchased letter opener.

Just like the silver bullet that had been shot from the gun of Samuel Galton, the previous carnation of Rosa, all those years ago that had killed Silas Hawkes. History had almost repeated itself except it had been Brooke who had dealt the blow in the twenty-first century. Nevertheless, it had taken Birmingham silver to kill the same person twice, so to speak. Silas and Vina.

But was Vina actually dead?

She certainly seemed to be.

Just then Judd walked into the carnage. "What the fuck has happened here?" he asked.

Errol spoke. "You've missed it all mate. Vina came in here and acted like a wild animal. She tried to kill Brooke but I'm glad to say that your lovely lady somehow managed to get the better of her."

Brooke? She would have been the last person who Judd would have expected to be at his FIGHT class today. "Brooke? What are you doing here? Are you ok?"

"No, Judd. I am far from fucking okay."

Judd turned his attention to Vina who had still not moved a muscle since the letter opener had entered her.

"Is she dead?" he asked.

"I fucking hope so," shouted Harper. "She almost

ripped my ear off."

"But…but," spluttered Judd.

"But what?" asked Sandy.

"She's erm, pregnant."

Brooke stared hard at Judd. "You really are a fucking bastard aren't you, Judd."

CHAPTER 36
LET IT BE

Stood on the banks of Great Barr Lake, Judd pulled up the collars of his overcoat to shield himself as much as possible from the biting chill. Apart from the odd ripple, the water stood practically still, which signified the coldness must have been in the air as opposed to a fierce, biting wind being in flight. Judd viewed a single white swan glide across the surface of the lake.

The lake had once belonged within the private grounds of Great Barr Hall, before forming part of the land of St Margaret's Hospital. These days it formed a pleasant feature of the mock-Georgian housing estate known as Nether Hall that had been constructed just beyond the silver birches, redwoods and pine trees. The foliage seemed to hug the banks of the lake like a huge protective arm. A small area of marshland stood at the northern tip where the water came to an end.

It was exactly three weeks to the day that he had attended Vina's funeral. He hadn't shed a tear for her but he had somehow felt obliged to pay his respects. Perhaps subconsciously he had needed an exact sense of closure to his relationship with Vina.

He had indeed sensed that the madness surrounding their relationship had been extinguished as he watched the curtain close on her coffin at the crematorium. Members of the City of Birmingham Symphony Orchestra had also attended, blissfully oblivious to Vina's double life, but the lack of family representation was telling.

As it turned out, Vina had lied about being pregnant. It had just been yet another example of her ability to twist people's emotions through her actions or words.

At least he had been spared a second unborn child of his being killed in their mother's womb.

The trouble was, Judd had kind of gotten used to the idea of being a father. Obviously, his natural choice of mother would have been his wife, Brooke, but any chance of a reconciliation was becoming increasingly slimmer by the day. He had let her down once too often and he painfully realised that this time his failing of her had been nothing short of catastrophic.

Way to go, Stone!

He hoped, but doubted, she would recover from the deep disappointment that she held for him.

Brooke had not been charged with Vina's murder. There had been far too many witnesses at the scene who had consistently confirmed that she had acted in a clear display of self defence.

It had been a little like history repeating itself, when the gathering who had been present at the killing of Silas Hawkes all those years ago, had also taken the oath that what had happened could only have been a reflection of them all. They had been in it together and were willing to share any responsibility. And keep any secrets.

Vina's funeral hadn't been the only one that Judd had attended recently. The remains of Martha Sadler, the missing scullery maid who had been found in the wall of Great Barr Hall, had finally been laid to rest in the grounds of St Mary's Church in nearby Handsworth, the exact same resting place as Lunar Society members James Watt and Matthew Boulton.

Judd now understood that the day that James Watt had met Matthew Boulton in 1768, carried a similar level of importance to the industrial world, as the day when John Lennon had met Paul McCartney in 1957 for the musical world.

Fellow Lunartick, William Murdoch had also been laid to rest in St Mary's Church. Therefore, following Martha's funeral, Judd had made a point of entering the church and laying flowers at the memorials of the three men who unbeknown to them had been an integral part of his journey over the past few months.

In the next few days, he would also ensure that he visited the graves of Frankie, William and Crystal.

Judd had now been able to conclude that the feelings of claustrophobia that Vina had been experiencing during her past life regressions had not occurred because she had been the one buried in Great Barr Hall. It had been Martha Sadler who had been unceremoniously positioned into that unbefitting resting place, and it had been Vina who had been responsible for that act during her carnation as Silas Hawkes.

Vina's feelings of claustrophobia must have been due to the perceived transformation of her body changing from Silas Hawkes into a werewolf type persona. The feeling of her body changing must have been agonising much like the transformation of humans into werewolves as depicted in various movies.

So that begged the question: Had Silas Hawkes been an actual bonafide werewolf? It was unlikely, Hawkes had messed with potions which could have easily altered his state of mind, but there again who would ever really know for sure?

Via all of the past life regressions that Judd knew had taken place, Matthew Boulton, as significant as he was, had been the only Lunartick who had failed to surface in the current lives of his circle of friends. This led him to consider if perhaps his old pal William Chamberlain had once been the industrial entrepreneur. They had similarities, not least they were both great men. If William had been around to undergo a past-life regression Judd certainly wouldn't have been surprised if his friend and mentor, with all his wisdom and intelligence, had once been the great inventor. Sadly, he perhaps would never know for sure.

Judd still missed his friend deeply, but he was satisfied that he had gone as far as he could in avenging his and Crystal's death. He realised that he had got closer than most to the hidden powers that truly operate large elements of the world's organised crime. At least those who had been directly responsible had been sufficiently punished.

During her time on earth, Crystal had been a medium, someone who had been able to make contact with the dead. This left Judd curious as to why Crystal had never reached out to him from the grave. Perhaps she simply couldn't reverse the roles now she was on the other side. He just hoped that both she and William were now both happy, but some kind of sign to confirm this would be welcoming.

Judd observed several Canadian geese break the surface of the water as they landed on it. As he watched the water begin to settle again, he pulled the memory stick from his pocket.

He knew that so many years of the Chamberlain's work was held on that stick but that was exactly it. It had been their work. He had no means of continuing what they had been researching and developing in the name of either science or spirituality. And he had discovered only too well what danger the contents of the stick could bring.

Judd hesitated and changed his mind countless times, wrestling with the decision to either abandon the important work of his dedicated friends or to keep hold of the stick and continue to be under threat from whatever danger it could attract. More importantly, the chances were likely that the contents of the stick would always present danger to others too.

His hesitating continued, but eventually Judd tossed the memory stick into the lake and watched the surface ripple as it instantly sank.

He had decided that although he couldn't bring William and Crystal back, he could however protect those that were still living. With the memory stick still around then the danger would have remained ever-present.

He just hoped that his two friends would have approved of his course of action. The contents of the memory stick had cost them their lives and almost Brooke's too, someone whom they had both been very fond of. So surely, they would have understood. Wouldn't they?

When a white feather fell from the sky, Judd was sure he had done the right thing. Judd had long accepted that the sudden presence of a white feather could indicate that those on the other side were reaching out to those still living in a bid to communicate. William and Crystal would have never wanted any harm to have come to him or Brooke.

As he looked up to see where the white feather may have come from, just as he expected, Judd could not see any bird flying overhead. This produced a smile of recognition on his face.

"Thank you, Crystal. Perhaps you have given me a sign after all. I trust you're ok wherever you are. How's things, William? God, I really miss you two guys."

Next, Judd caught sight of a cloud formation taking shape. He loved to do this as a kid. It was a method he deployed to help escape his demons. Back then he would lie on the grass, relax, and see what shapes the clouds forming in the sky would bring. The art of cloud watching had always been a useful distraction for him.

As he watched the clouds from the side of Great Barr Lake, he thought he could make out the shape of an anchor, or had it just been his mind looking for the interpretation of the Birmingham Assay marking which had been introduced by Matthew Boulton?

As the cloud quickly transformed into a more non-descript shape, it reminded Judd of what Gabriel Bolan had said to him. Paraphrasing the gangster's words in his mind it suddenly made perfect sense. The highest levels of organised crime were indeed untouchable, just like the clouds, just like the air. It reaffirmed his belief that Judd had indeed done as much as he could to avenge his friends.

Then, wanting to distance his mind from Bolan and everything else that had been toxic in recent times, Judd preferred to view the clouds as if they resembled steam. And on this scale, Judd decided that the clouds looked like the steam that could have come out of one of Boulton and Watt's steam engines of the industrial revolution. The legacy of the Lunar Society had been pretty amazing - in more ways than one - for Judd was now aware of their secrets too.

As Judd reflected further on both recent and historic events his concentration was broken by a recently acquainted voice.

The information on the memory stick had included a list of the Chamberlain's fellow employees and networks, many involved in applying scientific techniques. One particular person of note had been Dr Talbot Mackenzie who specialized in underwater forensics and Sound Navigation and Ranging systems. He was as accommodating as could be once he knew that Judd had been a mutual friend of William and Crystal. It turned out that Mackenzie had worked on many secret and controversial projects with the Chamberlains. Judd liked him instantly.

"We have located two distinct masses at the bed of the

lake."

"Two human bodies?" asked Judd.

"It's possible. The density of the masses would suggest they could be bodies, but we can't be sure. The only way of knowing for certain would be to bring whatever is down there up to the surface."

"There's really no other way of telling for sure?"

"I'm afraid not. It would also take some explaining as at this point, the students think this is just a training exercise. I've told them that some materials had been planted down there for training purposes only and I've praised them for finding them. Little do they know I actually had no idea what we would find. What do you want to do? It's your call, Judd."

"Only the two likely bodies?"

"Yes."

"It has to be them. It has to be Ada and Silas. I wondered if you may find more considering the history of this place, I had heard rumours that many a patient had gone missing from the hospital here."

"I'll assist you in whatever you want to do. Like I've already stated, I was used to providing support to William and Crystal in a variety of secret expeditions."

"You know what, Talbot? I see no point in scaring the horses and I've been to enough funerals of late. Can I ask you something?"

"Sure."

"If you had have been around in the eighteenth or nineteenth century, a guy like you could have easily been a member of the Lunar Society, right?"

"I'd like to think so. My methods and scientific techniques have been declared as being fairly ground breaking."

"So, what would people like Matthew Boulton and James Watt have done with this discovery do you think?"

Mackenzie stroked his beard as he pondered the question. "Hard to say. They were doing a lot of stuff to serve the common good and they had a direct positive impact on society. They were risk takers industrially but I'm not sure they were risk takers with people's emotions. If you pull these bodies out of the water what real good will it do? What can of worms will you be potentially opening?"

"Then in that case, I think I'll turn to the words of a more contemporary partnership of whose work I'm much more familiar with."

"Oh?"

"Yes, Talbot. Who am I to disturb the watery graves of two people who have found peace down there for the last few centuries?

"And who am I to cast any kind of shadow or controversy over the achievements of the Lunar Society?

"I've made my decision; Talbot and I think it's the right one. I'm going to let it be."

ABOUT THE AUTHOR

Martin Tracey is an author who likes to push the boundaries of reality. He lives in Birmingham, England and is married with two daughters. His passions include The Beatles and Wolverhampton Wanderers.

JUDD STONE WILL RETURN IN

Double Fantasy

MIND GUERRILLA

When a high-end escort is discovered murdered in her plush waterside apartment, so begins the hunt for a serial killer known as *The Crucifier* due to the unusual slaying and positioning of his victims.

In parallel there remains the need to locate a dangerous and elusive doomsday cult.

DCI William Chamberlain and DI Judd Stone have an acute thirst for justice on both accounts.

Stone is an ex-football hooligan turned cop. Riddled with guilt and anger, he is used to getting results – albeit somewhat unconventionally.

Chamberlain suffers from Multiple Sclerosis, but curiously, as his health deteriorates, his ability to perform acts of telekinesis increases. When faced with life or death, Chamberlain progresses from manipulating physical matter to controlling minds and sets in motion a dramatic chain of events.

But why do things spiral out of control, placing an unknown high-profile target in danger?

Assistance comes from the most unlikely of sources but who is also working against the wheels of justice?

And just what is the connection between *The Crucifier*, the cult and the high-profile target?

With Spaghetti Western overtones, the chase from Liverpool to London and through both Birmingham UK and Alabama, finds both detectives having to confront their darkest demons in pursuit of the sweet taste of revenge.

CLUB 27

DCI Judd Stone is heading for rock bottom. He breaks the rules, he gambles and he's begun to play around.

An unlikely lifeline is thrown Judd's way when he finds himself catapulted into trying to prevent Rock and Pop sensation Phoenix from becoming the next member of the infamous 27 club – the name given to the list of iconic musicians who die at the age of 27.

Judd's quest is not made easier when Phoenix's lifestyle is even more self-destructive than his own - but how can Judd possibly protect someone from themselves?

And who else could be conspiring to benefit from Phoenix's death? A crazed fan? Birmingham's ruthless Gangsters? A Secret Society? Or maybe even those who Phoenix believes to be closest to her?

And when Phoenix embarks on an unprecedented tour performing at some of the most wondrous places of the world, the stakes to protect her become even higher.

This sensational follow up to the award-winning *Mind Guerrilla* will have you rooting for the irrepressible Judd Stone all over again.